A Moth to the Flame

A Moth to the Flame

The Life of the Sufi Poet Rumi

CONNIE ZWEIG

ROWMAN & LITTLEFIELD PUBLISHERS, INC.
Lanham • Boulder • New York • Toronto • Plymouth, UK

ROWMAN & LITTLEFIELD PUBLISHERS, INC.

Published in the United States of America
by Rowman & Littlefield Publishers, Inc.
A wholly owned subsidiary of The Rowman & Littlefield Publishing Group, Inc.
4501 Forbes Boulevard, Suite 200, Lanham, Maryland 20706
www.rowmanlittlefield.com

Estover Road
Plymouth PL6 7PY
United Kingdom

Distributed by National Book Network

British Library Cataloguing in Publication Information Available

Library of Congress Cataloging-in-Publication Data

Zweig, Connie.
  A moth to the flame : the life of the Sufi poet Rumi / Connie Zweig.
    p. cm.
  ISBN-13: 978-0-7425-5243-2 (pbk. : alk. paper)
  ISBN-10: 0-7425-5243-8 (pbk. : alk. paper)
  1. Jalal al-Din Rumi, Maulana, 1207–1273. 2. Poets, Persian—Biography. I. Title.

PK6482.Z94 2006
891'.5511—dc22
[B]
                                                              2006027837

Printed in the United States of America

♾™ The paper used in this publication meets the minimum requirements of American
National Standard for Information Sciences—Permanence of Paper for Printed Library
Materials, ANSI/NISO Z39.48-1992.

Other books by Connie Zweig

To Be A Woman:
The Birth of the Conscious Feminine (Ed.)

Meeting the Shadow:
The Power of the Dark Side of Human Nature
(Ed. with Jeremiah Abrams)

Romancing the Shadow:
A Guide to Soul Work for a Vital, Authentic Life
(with Steve Wolf)

The Holy Longing:
The Hidden Power of Spiritual Yearning

Dedication

Ishq Allah Mahbud L'llah
God is love, the lover, and the beloved

For Neil
The one who wears the face of my beloved

For Andra Akers
sister in spirit
1945-2002

Author's Note

In the year 1207, in the rugged mountains of what is now Afghanistan, a boy was born to a mystical Muslim family who was destined to become the Shakespeare of the Islamic world. When the West discovered his work nearly eight hundred years later, at the turn of the millennium, he became the most popular poet in America – Jelaluddin Rumi.

In his homeland of Khorasan, a mountainous region east of the Mediterranean Sea, Muslims lived in peace with the other People of the Book, Christians and Jews. His city of Balkh on the Oxus River, which runs down from the Aral Sea, boasted thriving commerce, trade, and an environment of tolerance. Inhabitants believed that the neighboring town, Masar i Sharif, did not compare with Balkh. Nor did Samarkand to the north or Herat to the South. Balkh alone, they said, was the Dome of Islam.

A few years earlier, Muslim sultans had completed a conquest of Northern India. At the same time, Christian crusaders took Constantinople and established a Latin Empire. In 1214, Genghis Khan captured Peking for the Mongols. Three great cultures battled each other with devastating consequences.

In1215, hordes of Mongol archers on horseback approached Khorasan. At that time, the Muslim Empire was weak, divided from within: Sunnis, Shia, and Sufis of many orders vied for power and resources. Some believers called for their brothers to rise up and kill the infidel aggressors, justifying their hate and violence with the Koran. Others, like Balkh's Sultan Mohammed and his counselor, turned from Islam to Greek philosophy for answers and claimed that creation was made up of earth, air, water, and fire alone. For them, a belief in God's immanence was archaic superstition.

Even among the Sufis, or Muslim mystics, to the south in Kabul and to the far west in Constantinople, chaos reigned. Some men turned to music and dance – a heresy.

Jelaluddin's father, head of a large community, fled the attacks. Behind the departing caravan, Genghiz Khan and his hordes stampeded through Balkh, destroying it utterly. Rumi wandered, homeless, through the Persian empire for many years of his childhood. But exile is only the beginning of his journey. When he eventually finds home in Konya, Turkey, his spiritual homesickness begins.

Today, in the cross-fires of religious wars, each of us can find inspiration in his story: his anguish is our anguish, his victory, our potential victory, his transcendence, our hope.

People think they are born only once,
but they have been here so many times.
In the cloak of this ragged body
  I have walked countless paths.
With ascetics in the desert
  I watched night turn into day.
With pagans in the temple
  I slept at the foot of idols.
I've been a charlatan and a king;
I've been a healer, and fraught with disease.
I've been on my death-bed
  so many times. . . .

1

From my first breath I have longed for Him –
This longing has become my life.

1231 A.D.
Konya, Turkey

Pacing at the edge of the garden, his eyes burning, his lower lip trembling, he knows when he goes back inside his old life will be over. Dread surges into his mouth like a tart lemon, leaving it puckered and dry. Trudging back and forth in the chill to avoid the moment as long as he can, he shivers as the caftan flaps at his ankles and his sandals crunch the dirt.

Above him in the blackness, a comet shoots across the silver-dotted sky. *A bad omen?*

His stomach lurches when he notices that the red tulips, so loved by his father, have wilted. The queasiness passes and he begins pacing again, rubbing his palms together for warmth. But the wetness is seeping into the caftan now. He stops in his tracks, braces himself, and steps across the threshold into the house.

Pushing aside the curtain to his father's room, he peers in, and his stomach turns over again. The turbaned head of Bahaoddin rests on a worn, blue cushion. His beard, white with eighty snows, rests on his chest. He is lying still, his bronze face yellowed, his black eyes vacant, only his lips moving, murmuring the names of God.

Bending down over the patient to sniff his breath, the doctor seems troubled. Several days earlier, he prescribed bitter wood to improve appetite and anise to improve digestion. But Bahaoddin refused both. Now, the doctor urges his patient, "Master, rest for a minute. You can return to your practices soon."

1

His father arouses himself to reply. "All that I have gained is from these practices. I won't abandon them now." After nodding, the doctor exits the room.

As he moves closer to his father, folding his legs on the floor, he tugs at the bristles beneath his chin, the coarse clump of hair separating in his fingers. The women's voices in their quarters rise to a pitch, petitioning God to save the Master. He imagines them blowing on knots to appease the evil eye and mixing vinegar with the nectar of the hive to feed their *sheikh*.

A moment later, he hears a steed stomping outside the house. The sultan, bedecked in orange robes and gold earrings, hurries into the room and kneels low. "Master, Konya will not be the same without you."

"Don't be sad, sultan," Bahaoddin says in a hushed tone. "We come from God, and to God we return. You will follow me soon." Appearing frightened, the ruler scurries out.

Finally, his father turns his head toward him. "Before you came back, son, I had a dream, a conversation with the Holy One, who knows the future. There was a sultan, whose head was made of gold. His breast was made of silver, his body of bronze, his thighs of lead, his feet of pewter. As long as he was there, the people were as precious as gold. In the son's reign, they would be as precious as silver. After him, they would have the value of bronze."

The Master coughs, his chest rattling. He forces the words out. "Then a great disorder will arise. No sincerity, no faith in the fourth generation. By the fifth, the dynasty declines. The Mongols conquer the land."

The images chill him, as if he remains out in the night air. "But father, if we fight. . . ."

"Shhhhh. . . .The Brothers' safety from the Mongol hordes is in your hands now, son. Keep the people as precious as gold for as long as you can. Time is short."

The Brothers' safety. . . his duty?

Reaching beneath the carpets, his father pulls out a stack of papers that is bound between wooden boards. "You will need my teachings. Now they are yours," he murmurs, handing them over.

Choking back tears, he glances down – <u>The Divine Sciences</u> by Bahaoddin Velad -- and clutches the precious pages to his heart.

"And the final secret," Bahaoddin says under his breath. "Come closer." His father pulls the edge of his robe and draws him in, their beards touching, hot breath falling on his ear.

The whispered words startle him. Then Bahaoddin's head falls back on the pillow and he mutters, "In these terrible times, may God guide you on the path to Him as you guide our dervish Brothers."

No! Don't leave me, father. Mother is gone, not you now. Not yet. . .

Gulping down the scream, he blinks back tears and opens the pages of the book to distract himself from the rush of feelings. The curves and loops of the script seem to shine. *What of the hidden meanings and secret names that you have not told me? Are they here, on these pages, or will they die with you?*

His father's throat rattles. It's no time to read. As he sets the book aside, his glance returns to Bahaoddin.

The old man's skin, once smooth as an urn, is creased and furrowed now. His hollow eyes, looking weary, slowly withdraw. The names of God grow fainter on his lips and finally cease altogether. Silence.

A wave of grief rolls through him, threatening to overtake him, as he turns his father's turbaned head toward Mecca and prepares him for resurrection on judgment day. Then he hears himself say, "There is no god but God."

An instant before, he was a son, a disciple. Now he is alone. He can no longer look up into Bahaoddin's wise, fearless face. He can no longer pose any question and expect to be escorted through the arguments until he knows the correct response. For the first time, he is without a true friend, without a guide.

The grief gives way to shock as he stands up to leave the room. His mind is racing. *How could this have happened? I am twenty-four and the only link in a chain of teachers going back to the Prophet.*

After the family and disciples bid farewell to the Master, he watches the Brothers wash the body, stuff the ears, nose, and mouth with cotton, tie the ankles together, rest the hands on the chest, and wrap his father in a linen shroud. As they carry the corpse on a bier past shops and mosques, the people of Konya, rich and poor, Muslim and Christian, follow in procession, their heads uncovered. Tearing their robes to shreds until their bodies are nearly bare, they cry out verses from the Koran, the psalms, the gospels. The *muezzin's* rising chants fill the air with song as his heart wells up with grief.

Arriving at the grave in the rose garden, the Brothers set down the bier on the earth, and he moves forward tentatively, out of the crowd. Just then, a distraught disciple throws himself on the bier, shouting, "I'm going with you. I want to enter paradise with you, Master."

His heart aches for the man and he knows exactly what he feels. He too has lost his direction and longs to join his father in paradise, to be embraced in the arms of Allah.

But it is his duty now to comfort the Brothers, to offer them guidance, to explain their larger purpose. With the others watching, he links his arm through the man's elbow and lifts him up to standing, saying, a bit meekly, "Have a passion for life, not death, Brother."

But his heart resists his own words, demanding, *What is there to live for without the loving presence of my father? Who am I, if not his son?*

Attempting to shake off the hopelessness for the sake of the believers, he continues, "Brothers, instead of following death, enter the greater life. Marry your own soul, as my father did. That is our deeper purpose." And he knows in that moment that he speaks as much to himself as to the grieving disciple.

Following the funeral, he remains by the tomb as distraught dervishes in blue robes, mouthing prayers and shedding tears, gather among the red and yellow roses. Men stroke the circular stone and its conical cap with long fingers, praying for the Master's intercession in their lives. Scarved women kneel and sob gently, leaving bundles of *halva* in exchange for wishes granted. A young girl places a yellow rose against the stone. Finally, only he is left standing. Alone.

The next afternoon, as the sun rolls overhead, he drapes himself in his father's black robe with the wide sleeves, the gown of a scholar. And he makes his way up the hill toward the great mosque as if for the first time. Below him, off to one side, green fields of lettuce and strawberries stretch as far as he can see. Off to the other, golden grains of wheat sway in the breeze. The silver dome covers the rectangular building like the dome of heaven itself. Long-necked white storks nest in the two silver minarets, which soar high into the blue sky. Slipping off his shoes, he crosses the threshold.

Inside, thick, carved marble columns support arched passageways. A wooden stairway carved with linking lines that form stars leads to the pulpit, inlaid with mother-of-pearl. Flaming red carpets cover the floors between the pillars.

As he steps up to the pulpit, four Koran reciters surround him, and the people seated before him now believe that the Prophet Mohammed, blessed be he, addresses them today through him, their *sheikh. And yet. . . .*

He may be intellectually prepared, having studied the Koran and the intricacies of Muslim law. He has read widely in philosophy – Ghazzali who, paralyzed and mute from a loss of faith, claimed that practices, not theological arguments, would fulfill the promise of religion. Suhrawardi, who urged believers to make a symbolic, not a literal reading of the Koran. And Ibn 'Arabi in Spain, who proclaimed that each individual is a unique expression of a divine attribute of God.

Besides Persian, he speaks Arabic and Turkish. He knows how to work with numerals and to recognize Capricorn, the mountain goat, and Sagittarius, the archer with the long tail of a dragon, in the night skies. *But what does it all add up to?*

His father, wise in the hidden meanings, passed on only a few secrets to him. Spiritually, he is unprepared, a novice. He has knowledge of Sufism, but not experience. He knows about God, but he has not seen Him face to face.

Setting his hands firmly on his father's worn copy of the Koran, he surveys the sea of eager faces: the sultan in a red gown with the weaver, butcher, candle maker, tanner, perfume seller, and stonecutter in threadbare robes. Some men bow their heads and move their lips in constant *zikhr*. Clustered in the rear, women in headscarves pulled across their mouths begin to sway back and forth in silence. A neighboring *sheik* in a coiled, green turban sits beside a Christian monk, who hides his light skin in a black cowl. The Jewish wine seller is bareheaded. And an adolescent boy in billowing white robes, oblivious of the crowd, wanders up and down between the pillars, grinning at something the others cannot see.

As hundreds of eyes bore through his robe, he feels naked. His father no longer stands between him and the peoples' great hunger. He draws a breath and does the only thing he can do, the duty that is required of him at this moment: he praises God, blesses the Prophet, offers blessings to the sultan, and begins his first discourse as the *sheikh*.

"Brothers," he begins, "why do we open each prayer with a negation? 'There is no God,' we say, 'but God,' we affirm. We negate the world, then we affirm the existence of God."

The power of mystery seems to enter the room, and he is encouraged to go on, a bit louder. "Don't listen to these words. Listen behind them. Words are a shadow of reality. A resonance draws one man to another, not words. If a man sees a thousand miracles but there is no resonance connecting him with that *sheikh*, then those phenomena will be useless."

He pauses, regarding his listeners. "If there is no amber in a straw, the straw will not move toward amber. If there is no resonance in a man, he will not move toward a *sheikh*."

He clears his throat. He has known these truths for so long that the words ring hollow to him. His tongue feels thick. As he studies the people, a few glare at him like an idol, a dazzling peacock to adore. For an instant, his chest puffs up. *Yes, my mind is quicker than theirs, my heart more faithful.*

After pausing, he comes back to himself. *No, I will not accept their worship. I am merely their guide, their caravan leader.*

But this knowledge and position are not enough for him. They are not who he is. Even the sacred law, ablutions, prayers, alms, and fasting do not satisfy his hunger. They, too, come and go like joy or sadness.

A restless yearning is arising in him again, gnawing at him, and demanding something more from life, more than this fleeting outer form.

What is this longing that calls me away from duty and gives me no peace? I will go through the motions, but one day I will have to heed the call, turning toward what I most deeply love, in spite of any danger, any risk.

He reins in his impatience and attends to his followers. "Every thing other than God is leading you astray, be it your throne, kingdom, or crown. The world's harp has but a single string."

An expectant hush comes over the crowd. Some stare up at him, rapture on their faces. Others hang their heads, weeping with reassurance. Even the restless children are quieted. With this sermon, the hundreds of disciples of his father are now devoted to him.

From this day forward he is called Rumi, named after Rum, the land of Roman Anatolia in south central Turkey on which he stands. He wraps himself in the name, and it settles on his shoulders like a cloak. It ties him to the land, its fortunes, and its fate. He is no longer Jelaluddin of Balkh. He is the *sheikh* of Rum.

But in his inmost heart, he longs for something more, something that is untouched by these comings and goings. And this gnawing feeling leaves him restless and thirsty.

2

From a distance you tremble with fear –
Can't you see the mighty warrior
*   standing ready in your heart?*

On the first dawn of the forty-day mourning period for his father, Rumi sits alone in his reception room. His mother's carpet with red roses covers the East wall and a stack of books lies horizontally in a niche beneath it. A water jug stamped with wavy script and a small bronze bowl stand beside them. A piece of fabric woven with a design of vines and grapes hangs behind him, separating the room from a corridor.

Rumi feels God reach out to him, and his own longing awakens. He lifts his hands beside his head, palms open, and cries out to Him. Placing his hands on his knees, he bows low. Again, he comes to standing for a breath, then cries out, "God is great," plunging into prostration, resting his forehead on the carpet.

As a gentle light lifts the veil of darkness, a veil lifts from his heart. Just then, a guest knocks at the door, jarring him. Reluctant to receive anyone, he hesitates. But hospitality is a duty. His time alone is over.

Muinoddin Pervane, the sultan's emir, a stocky man with a sparse beard, greets him at the door, "*Asalaam alaykum*, Master," and bows to kiss his hand.

Master? The word sends a shock wave through him as he feels the strangeness of lips brushing the back of his hand for the first time.

He gestures to Pervane to take a seat on the cushions as he goes to light the oil lamps, which sputter and flicker. Realizing that Pervane awaits permission to speak, he nods toward him.

"Master, the Mongols are coming closer now."

As he seats himself across from the visitor, alarm surges through his body, and he pulls on the strands of beard on his cheek. *Father's prophecy, so soon.*

Pervane continues. "It started when Genghiz Kahn's merchants were murdered by a Seljuk governor. The Khan sent messengers demanding the recall of the governor, who returned those men with their beards shaved off! In retaliation, the Khan laid siege to the governor's town. When he finally surrendered, the Mongols poured molten silver into his eyes and ears until the sights and sounds of this world vanished forever. Such is the revenge of Genghiz Khan."

Rumi recoils, staring at the carpet's red rose as the messenger's words rush on. "The Accursed One moved his troops to Bukhara, where they turned libraries into stables and made litter of the pages of the Koran! The infidels went on to Nishapur, Heart, and Merv, turning city after city to cinder.

"Then the sultan got word he was dead. We thought the reign of terror would end, God willing. But no," Pervane swallows hard, "don't believe it if someone tells you the Mongols have suffered a defeat! The Khan divided his empire among four sons, who shrewdly converted to Islam – but they didn't truly submit."

His heart pounds like a drum in his chest as he tries to imagine a false conversion to the faith. He wipes his wet forehead, struggling to find suitable words. "How many believers have suffered at the hands of these hordes! But no matter what the Mongols or the Christians destroy, the five pillars of Islam live on in every Muslim, *insh'allah,* God willing."

"But we must free the empire of the infidels!" the emir insists, slamming a fist into a cushion. "We must rid the world of them on behalf of Allah."

"Yes, well. . . I will ask God for His direction, and we will see." He stands to let the man out.

Rumi's mind is a jumble of thoughts. *Father, what should I do? Flee as you did from our homeland or protect the Brotherhood in some other way? Those Mongols wander about breeding cattle and living in round tents, their doorways marked by silken idols. They worship the sky and the*

rivers, and their code, their Godless yasa, *extols nothing but power. It permits them to get drunk three times a month!*

Then he remembers Bahaoddin's final gift. Perhaps he can find guidance there. In the bedroom, he takes <u>The Divine Sciences</u> from a wall niche, opens to a random page, and reads a line aloud. "To make a decision, to quiet the mind from distractions, seek help from God the guide by chanting the secret name *al-Hadi*."

Collapsing to the floor, he leans back against the wall. Following a sigh of relief, he draws in his breath, closes his lids, and begins to chant *al-Hadi, al-Hadi* again and again, his body calming, his agitation quieting. *Al-Hadi, al-Hadi.*

3

Laugh at those faithless men
who boast with loud voices.
Weep for that friend
who has turned away from the Friend.

Rumi's mind drifts, wandering off the divine name, returning to that day long ago, that turning point moment in his life. At eight years old, he is sauntering down the lane to the mosque beside Bahaoddin, skipping in and out of a dark quivering shape in the dirt cast by his father's high turban and long, swinging caftan. At last, he is leaving the women's quarters to attend his first *zikhr*, to learn how to chant with the men. The distant mountain peaks of Khorasan glow, darkening as they descend toward earth. Slowly, the pointed tops of the minarets come into view, and his excitement grows.

They join other dervishes in front of four baked-brick buildings grouped around a courtyard and covered with a single gray dome. Awaiting the call to prayer, the men chat among themselves, their hands gesturing, their turbans bobbing. At the arched entrance, he feels dwarfed by the slim tower that spirals toward the sky. From one of its balconies, a *muezzin* calls to the faithful, "There is no God but God. Mohammed is His messenger. Come to prayer, come to the highest realization."

As his father and the others pass under the arch, he enters the courtyard too, holding his breath. He has envisioned this moment, standing before the vine-covered courtyard fountain, with its large stone tank and waterspouts, the scent of honeysuckle hanging in the air. And here he is.

"You must come to God clean, Jelaluddin," Bahaoddin tells him, "washed of dirt and desires, no other wish than to serve God's will," as he passes his wet hand over his face and head and splashes his arms with the water.

Scooping water over his arms, neck and face, Jelal tries to imagine the cool liquid diluting his desires, washing away the pride he feels about joining the men at the mosque. He does not know whether the same water that quenches his thirst can clean his heart, as well as his face and hands. But his father believes it, and his father's father. So, it must be true.

While Bahaoddin lingers in the courtyard, he enters the prayer hall with the others, who are folding their knees on colored carpets in rows that face a square niche, which indicates the direction of Mecca to the south. A bronze lamp, whose perforated form allows light to shine through it, hangs over the niche. *Ah, the light. . . the light of Allah*, he sighs.

As the men await the entrance of their *sheikh*, an air of anticipation gives way to a gentle calm, which blankets the group. When they are perfectly still, his father comes through the doorway without making a single gesture to disturb the air.

"To exist is to pray." Bahaoddin's voice is born of the silence. The trees bow in ritual prayer, and the birds sing their litany, his father continues. As the Koran says, we are those men who are not diverted by trading or selling from prayer or *zikhr*, remembrance of God. We are those men who keep the names of God between our teeth. That is the real task of Sufis, the lovers of God in the Muslim brotherhood, to repeat His name with every breath.

Today, in the year 1215, he says, there are growing numbers of Sufis in Persia, Egypt, even India. Our sober Brothers strive to fulfill His commands, but we have a love affair with Allah. They focus on outer behavior – prayers, fasting, giving alms, making the pilgrimage to Mecca, and interpreting the Koran in strict ways. But we focus more on the inner life, purifying our feelings of lust and greed, the furnace of desire. We read the Koran as if it's full of signs and hidden meanings, a mystery to be unveiled within us.

Bahaoddin pauses, looking around intently at the group. And our Shiite brothers, he adds, shaking his head, with their devotion to Ali and their claim of the only true faith. And their infallible *imam*, who is clashing now with our sultan. May we learn to live together in peace, he concludes, indicating with his hands for the men to rise.

They stand and form straight lines, their shoulders touching in silence. Jelaluddin is struck by the physical similarity of the men: dark-haired and olive-skinned, with great, bushy beards, and long robes or woolen vests. Some tie their turbans with black or green. Others tie them with white. But all of them move about restlessly, their eyes darting here and there.

His father towers above them, his chocolate-brown skin streaked with gray shadows, his velvety eyes at rest, his jaw relaxed, his hands falling on his robes. His turban stands taller and fuller than the others to indicate his rank.

Bahaoddin continues, "We are Allahis. Let us repeat Allah, the divine name of God, riding the breath like a bird to freedom from earth's fetters. Allah, Allah, Allah. . ." his voice rings out, emphasizing the first part of His name.

The men chime in, their voices slowly attuning to one another until they sing the name of God as one voice. "Allah, Allah, Allah. . ."

Between breaths, Jelal recalls the words of the Prophet: a faithful believer standing near to a faithful believer is like the bricks of a wall enforcing each other. And he understands. He feels his faith reinforced by the faith of his brothers in that room and rests contentedly for a moment.

But, just then, a Sufi novice wearing the twisted green turban of another Order comes forward, approaching Bahaoddin, breathing in great gulps. "*Asalaam alaykum*, Master," he mumbles, hanging his head in deference.

"And peace on you, my brother. You are disturbed?"

"I have bad news to report. Temuchin, leader of the Mongol invaders, attacked Reyy, rousting the believers from their underground houses and slaughtering them. He commanded his armies to destroy our cities so the world can become a great steppe in which Mongol mothers suckle their children."

Jelal's calm is past, and a disturbance fills the room. His father is clenching a fist and releasing it again.

The messenger presses on. "Temuchin is now called Genghiz Khan. He has a voice of thunder and the hands of a bear. He eats a

15

whole sheep every day and drinks huge quantities of mare's milk. They say he buries his dead men seated in their tents before tables of meat, along with a horse and mare for life in the next world."

The speaker pauses. "Master, his only pleasure is to vanquish his enemies. And he leads his armies toward us now, thousands of them."

His father, frowning, dismisses the messenger, addressing the men gathering around him. "I need to be alone to contemplate this news. Return to your families and we'll meet here tomorrow. Until then, God be with us."

As Bahaoddin hurries out of the mosque, Jelal trails behind him. Moving past their neighbors' mud-brick houses, his father reassures him that, despite their differences, these are our people. They donate one-fifth of their prosperity each year to those in need. They obey the law of hospitality, offering food and shelter to any guest. And they study the Koran.

Bahaoddin and Jelal pass a Buddhist cloister, where two red-robed monks with shaven heads sit carving a large piece of wood across their knees. At the Jewish temple, three men in flat, black skullcaps flail their arms in heated debate. For years these people have lived in peace beside their Muslim brothers, Bahaoddin tells him. But now the Mongols, who rip open the bellies of live animals and hold their beating hearts in their hands, are coming, wishing to slaughter them all.

Jelal shudders as his father slows his pace at the central square where the Wednesday bazaar is held. The traders are gone, and the doors to the *souk* are shut. Turning left off the square toward home, Bahaoddin hastens then, approaching another mosque with nine domes and intricately carved brick arches. As they come near the two soaring, circular minarets, girdled with balconies, he slows down, his hand on his heart.

"Even if captured by the Mongols, I will not betray Islam. Whatever happens, I will be in the hands of God. As God has put His trust in me, so will I trust in Him."

Jelaluddin feels the power of his father's vow soothing him.

When they arrive home, where sweet peas climb the walls and cucumber vines trail in the dirt, they enter the reception area, which is scented with burning wild rue seed. After crossing the cooking area, they wait at the curtain to his mother's room, taking in the hanging carpet on the wall, its hand-woven, delicate pattern of roses, the prayer rugs, rolled up and piled neatly to one side, and the bundles of clothes stored in wall niches. Simple order, the way she likes it.

Mumine, humming to herself, is slowly folding a cloth, oblivious to events. She turns, smiling, toward them, her cheeks dimpling. Nodding to her, Bahaoddin signals with an index finger that he is going up to the rooftop terrace and climbs the ladder.

When his father returns several hours later, he tells Jelal about his contemplation. While Bahaoddin stood facing Mecca, a bitter wind swept through his robes. Chanting the names of God, he heard a voice say, "If you don't want to be with Me, you will always be restless and lost. But if you want to be with Me, then the place does not matter. I am with you wherever you are."

Then a vision appeared before his inner eye: red flames raged through his mosque until it was gutted and crumbled to ruins. The minaret toppled like a dying beast. Women ran through the streets, their arms flailing, their uncovered hair blowing in the gray, sooty air. Some men hurried about in search of weapons to protect their families. Others, too stunned to move, waited, paralyzed, before their houses, their mouths open.

When Bahaoddin's mind was blank at last, he tried to rest, awaiting the first thread of light. He knew then what he had to do.

Hours later, arriving at the mosque to tell the Brothers the news, father and son enter the domed prayer hall. Turbaned men fold their knees on the carpet between the columns, the oldest near to Bahaoddin and the youngest off to the side. The sultan, draped in an orange caftan, sits in the front surrounded by his advisers. Several women squat in the rear, their mouths covered by the corners of their headscarves.

To the right of the prayer niche, Bahaoddin mounts the stair to his pulpit and opens his arms, his sleeves falling like two large, black feathers. After praising Allah and blessing the Prophet, he halts. Instead of preaching from the Koran by memory, when words flow from him like water, he places it on a carved wooden stand and begins in a soft voice, "Beware, Sultan Mohammed and the people of Balkh, I foresee great dangers here."

He clenches his fists and lets them fall to his sides. "The hordes of Mongol infidels are coming. Soon Balkh will lie in ruins."

A rumble rises, and his speech grows louder as the words begin to spill out of him. "Beware, all that you have built, the great mosques and minarets, the piles of *dinars* you have amassed in your cellars – it is fleeting."

Fear pulses through the hall. Several members of the sultan's court storm out of the room. Merchants get up and huddle at the back, whispering among themselves. A few dervishes pale and move forward to be closer to Bahaoddin. The women pout, resting their cheeks in their palms.

Jelal wants desperately to help his father, to send him support somehow, but doesn't know what to do.

"Master," the carpet maker is on his feet, "this is such a drastic decision – I. . ."

Bahaoddin just shakes his head. "Brothers, it is time to depart. God has shown me the danger, and He has shown me the way. If you stay, you will die."

"I won't leave!" a merchant roars, rising up. "Like Saladin taking back Jerusalem from the Crusaders, we must make *jihad* against the infidels. Allah will reward us in paradise."

The words cast a pall over the crowd. His father bows his head for a moment. "Behind me the Mongol soldiers are coming, spreading over the world like locusts. I am departing. May God take pity on all of you who stay here, for you will taste the bitterness of death."

Al-Hadi, al-Hadi. . . . the divine name bobs back into Rumi's awareness and floats out again.

In grief and fear, they leave Balkh, wandering in caravan for seven years, homeless. Early in the exile, the pigeon post brings the news: a half million Mongols sacked and razed Balkh, reducing it to ruins. Two hundred thousand men and boys were shot through with arrows, hundreds of mosques burned down, thousands of copies of the Korans torched. Sultan Mohammed fled, with Genghiz Khan's son in hot pursuit. Bahaoddin's vision, granted by God, came to life.

Now, after five years of peace in Konya, the infidels are closing in again. Peace, so fleeting.

And this time, the decision is his. To take up arms and wage a battle. . . to flee and enter exile again. . . or to stay and place the Brothers in grave danger. . .

Al-Hadi, al-Hadi. . . . In response to his prayer, a plan begins to form in his mind.

4

The dervish who gives away
        the secret teachings, and all he owns,
that dervish lives by the grace
        of someone else's hand.

Shamsoddin of Tabriz does not dream the dreams of other men. He does not yearn to caress a woman's skin. He does not imagine holding an innocent babe in his arms or watching a son grow as straight and tall as a cypress. And he does not share the passion of Islam's warriors for saving the empire from Christian infidels.

His sun-baked, craggy face mapped like the dry Anatolian plains, his skull and eyebrows shaven smooth as a gourd, Shams wears an odd felt hat that rises to several points and bears the words, *No God but God*, emblazoned on it. From beneath the hat his eyes flare.

In draping, tattered robes, caked with the reds and browns of road dust, he wanders the steppe, its prickly scrubs and sparse grasses unyielding beneath his feet. And he carries only a massive carved staff, no food, no money, no Koran, practicing absolute trust in Allah, the One who nourishes.

But Shams does carry a single, burning desire: to find his beloved, a true friend of God, and commune with him. To become intoxicated with the wine of love, and to bring this worthy soul step by step to God. Only then will his destiny be fulfilled.

During the five-times daily prayer and in continuous dialogue with the divine, he cries out, "In the name of God, the infinitely Compassionate and Merciful, I, Shams of Tabriz, ask Your help. Let me meet Your true friend. Let me see an ocean in a drop. That is all I ask." And the heat of this desire has scorched all other desires and burned them away until he has become that -- the seeker of the spiritual friend -- and that alone.

This spiritual friend will have mastered the *nafs*, those animal passions that take men away from Him. He will have killed off the rooster of lust, the peacock of fame, and the crow of ownership, and turned them into another wanting, a divine desire. And he will pierce the veil of appearances to see into Shams, tolerating his fierceness and easing his solitude. *Together we will mirror the lover and the beloved to one another, an undisturbed reflection on polished metal.*

For nearly forty years, Shams has traipsed from the cool shade of conifer forests near the Black Sea and the parched heat of sandy wastelands in southern Arabia to the great cities of Persia, to Baghdad, Shiraz, Samarkand, Mecca, and Constantinople, seeking his friend. He leans into the warm, whistling wind and submits to being pulled forward toward an unknown center. Shams, whose name means the Sun, seeks the center of the universe, the orb around which he can circle.

He has carried this desire for so long, first as a blessing from God Himself, then as a curse of the dark angel, that it has become his only reason to live. Now, nothing else stirs him, not food, not fear, not learning, not prayer. Only the faith that he will find a true friend of God.

As a young man in Tabriz, Shams receives initiation from a basket weaver, a lover of Allah. This man does not see into him or recognize his spiritual abilities, so Shams is not able to commune with him but, rather, feels alone in his presence.

However, the basket weaver gives him a gift, telling him that man is not sinful but forgetful. For this reason, he needs to repeat the names of God in remembrance.

Whispering al-'Alim, God the Knower, again and again, Shams' stormy mind quiets, becoming as still as a lake, and he tastes *fana*, his animal passions extinguished. Soon after, his appetite for food disappears, and his need for rest lessens, until he sleeps for only two or three hours each night. As he leaves behind the temptations of the world, the greed of merchants and the lust of married men, he wants only union with Him.

During that time, he memorizes the Koran, inhaling slowly and reciting the *suras* in long phrases during the exhalation. Until, one evening, the verses continue to sing even during his dreams. But they do not bring contentment and, eventually, leave his mouth dry.

Seeking greater masters to transport him to higher spiritual stations, at age forty he goes to Shiraz in search of Razi, a disciple of Najmuddin Kubra, the Sculptor of Saints. Razi teaches him how to control his breath and hold certain postures while chanting the divine names. Shams practices for long hours, becoming absorbed in utter stillness, until his mind sinks into the well of the heart, and a numinous green light fills the well.

When he tells Razi about this experience in order to gain further guidance, the master doubts him, saying that such a beginner could not attain that spiritual station so quickly. Again, a *sheikh* fails to recognize the signs in him. Again, the disappointment, the loss. Unable to trust anyone to guide him further, he chooses to trust in God alone.

Now in his sixtieth year, he is outside Baghdad as the sun pitches its shining tent over the city. He sits beneath a tall, twisted cypress, folds his legs beneath him, and closes his lids. *Fana!* His lower self dissolves quickly, and his mind dives into an ocean of silence. Deeper, deeper into the silence until the wanting animal that lives in the body loosens its grip. Absolute quiet surrounds and embraces him, and he merges with it. *This wine was never held in a stone jar.*

The sweetness still on his lips, he stretches out his legs to release the stiffness behind his knees and rests back on his hands, which sink into the prickly grass. Then he pulls his legs beneath him again, cups his palms in his lap, and sinks into the vast silence. He can move in and out of *fana* as easily as moving from waking to dreaming and back again.

But, at dusk, his single desire surfacing ferociously once more, he enters Baghdad empty-handed. The capital overflows with refugees driven from their homes by the Mongol invasions. Simple tents, pitched next to elaborate, many-domed mosques, were bursting with the cries and chortles of children. Men in turbans and colorful caftans and women wrapped and veiled in black stroll about aimlessly. Donkeys and camels wander the streets, turning up dust, as the men who lead them try to trade goods for food.

Circling the round city of Sultan Nasir's palace, with its manicured grasses spreading across the west bank of the reed-lined Tigris, Shams steps on fallen palm fronds, which crunch beneath his feet. The air is perfumed with jasmine and rose.

Years earlier, Shams entered the ruler's court and saw the hanging cloths of violet silk with shining brocade flowers, the elaborate pillows of red and green silks, the wall niches filled with colored earthenware vases. He observed black eunuchs serving feasts to the sultan, who was decked in gowns of gold, and a cloaked scribe with reed pen in hand, standing ready to take down his every word.

Now, Shams keeps his sight averted from the sinful sultan. *Nasir is a scholar of the law, yet he lives in luxury while his subjects starve, unable to pay the price of bread. In daylight he feigns holiness, while at night he has sodomy with children in the dark.* Disgust rises up in him like the taste of a bitter turnip.

"*Asalaam alaykum.*" A warrior of the faith, who vowed to struggle against evil and protect Islam, tries to attract his attention with the wave of an arm.

The archer's quiver of arrows and two-pointed sword hanging through a belt do not interest him. "Peace on you," he nods, turning away.

As he comes around a corner into a crowded street, an Islamic scholar in black robes and a white turban approaches and, standing before him, attempts to draw him into a debate. "Friend, two members of my mosque committed adultery, the infidels! And the judge sentenced them to a mere hundred lashes. I want them stoned to death! You look like a believer. Tell me, can I count on you for support?"

Shams bristles. The legal arguments of the black-and-white makers leave his mind flat. "Not now."

Those Islamic scholars seeking answers, hunters seeking deer, priests seeking converts, they are all the same: in search of phantoms. They know nothing of the one taste of fana, *the unity of life. Even those Muslims who claim to be more pious than others want praise for their religious piety! But*

24

all sense of individuality is a curse. All separateness, the essential cause of human suffering.

He continues through the city streets, the clamor rising, until he stands before a Turk who sits astride an embroidered saddle on a high-backed, wiry pony, whose dyed red tail swats swarming flies. Shams meets the rider's gaze, assesses him quickly and moves on.

A while later, on the street of the booksellers, he passes the House of Wisdom, where scholars have penned thousands of manuscripts in elegant calligraphy. On his last visit, he witnessed learned Muslims, Christians, Jews, and even men from the East debating the fine points of philosophy and recording their arguments on thin, rough paper, unlike the scholars of Europe, who still write on parchment. Their books describe the celestial movements of stars, the Greeks' elemental medicine, new theories of optics and germs, the biographies of men with their physical and intellectual lines of descent, and various guides to interpret dreams as messages from God. But today Shams does not feel the pull of knowledge.

As the canopy overhead turns from blue to black, he still strides through the streets imploring both God and men to show him the way to his friend. "Can you show me a man of God, one who has attained a high spiritual station?"

"You need to see *sheikh* Kermani." A woman in an orange robe and green shawl points down a side road toward a *medrasa*. Shams leaps in that direction and enters a tree-lined courtyard, moving toward the central fountain and the renowned *sheikh*, his breath suspended.

5

The Sufi's book is not composed of ink and letters:
It is naught but a heart white as snow.

To put his plan into action, Rumi must visit the sultan, Aloeddin Kaykobad. From his house, the palace is an hour's walk. Gliding through ranks of cypress and pine, he recalls what his father told him about the ruler, who is faithful to their Order.

"When Aloeddin Kaykobad's brother was sultan, he imprisoned him to hold onto power. Alone for years, Aloeddin dreamed of building towns where religious leaders, poets, and artisans could work in peace, safe from Crusaders on one side and Mongols on the other. When his brother died in 1219, he set out to reclaim cities from the infidels and to link them with guesthouses a day's march apart by camel caravan.

"Kaykobad chose Konya for its special history: it was the first place to emerge after the great flood. When St. Paul preached here, it was known as Iconium. Taking it over, Aloeddin built a strong army and a prospering town. But the ruler believed that the city was incomplete without me, his Master. So he offered to build a great *medrasa* if I would come teach there."

For Rumi, settling in Konya meant leaving life in the caravan. It also meant leaving his mother's grave by the cypress tree in Armenia. But he loved the city from that first day, when they crossed a drawbridge to the sound of hooves clattering and entered the gates. Sultan Kaykobad slid down from his black steed and reached out to kiss Bahaoddin's hand, but his father extended his staff instead. And the sultan of the world bent his knee to kiss the staff of the sultan of the spirit.

In that instant Rumi felt at home, as he does now, entering a dark alleyway where green-eyed cats roam and coming out into a square where a male gypsy in a tattered red vest and pointed shoes blocks his path. The man's silver earrings catch the sunlight. His wife, her head wrapped in a red and orange scarf, squats in front of several colorful cards lying on the ground. Peering up at him, she asks, "Read your fortune?"

"No, our fortune is in the hands of Allah. May He bless you and protect you." With his right hand over his breast, he sinks the other into his robe, pulls out a coin, and offers it to the gypsy.

"Thank you, Master," he says, nodding.

Passing the bathhouse, its disrobing chamber and cold and hot water rooms, he moves toward the outskirts of the city. Earthen ovens jutting from mud walls line the road. He slows to watch workers making mud bricks, the building blocks of the city, realizing that the earth itself is shaped to form houses, schools, even mosques.

Three men, their turbans stained with sweat, pull wood from a pile and chop it into sticks. Another, his face creased with grime, shoves the sticks into an oven as a trail of gray smoke rises. Two others scoop dirt and clay from the earth, wet it down, pack it into wooden frames, and shove them into the oven. An Arab wearing a black and white scarf around his head and neck loads a pile of finished, reddish bricks onto a donkey-drawn cart.

Suddenly, he is aware of the rumbling drumbeat of horse hooves getting louder. Five riders on silver-gilded saddles, armed with bows and arrows, their capes fluttering, their bodies in seamless motion with their long-necked horses, sweep past without slowing down. Their eyes are narrow slits beneath their brows, their noses wide, their necks short and thick. And their long, stringy beards seem to fly in the breeze.

Through a tornado of dust, Rumi hears a brick-maker growl, "It is the Mongol infidels from the East. May God forsake and destroy them."

"Dirty dogs," gripes another. "They never dip their hands into water! They never wash their clothes!"

"Before long, there will be no safe place for true believers," the first man retorts. "Infidels and fanatics everywhere!"

With rising trepidation, Rumi lunges ahead. *The vast empire is squeezed at each end: Christian knights invading from the West. Archer infidels invading from the East. What will become of Islam?*

Passing through the first gate to the sultan's palace, he traverses a spacious, deserted courtyard, crosses it to another gate, and enters a vaulted corridor, which is divided into sections by tall arches. Moving beneath the arches into a smaller courtyard, he finds a line of robed men crouching against a crumbling wall, waiting to make or answer charges to the sultan.

Rushing past them, he arrives at the bottom of a long stair to the palace entrance, and his eyes move upward. The building is covered with glazed tiles in hexagonal and cross shapes, which fit together perfectly. He sets his aim on a massive, carved wooden door and climbs up, two steps at a time. The servant who answers leads the way to the ruler, who is seated on a throne beneath a triple archway, surrounded by members of his court. On seeing him, the sultan rises and escorts him out of the room.

They ascend to a terraced roof to observe the massive city wall, whose stones are signed in gold by every builder, and the many lookout towers above the moat, where guards are posted to protect the city from invasion.

"A city without a wall is like a blade without a sheath," Kaykobad boasts.

Rumi knows the ruler is trying to reassure him of their safety. "Yes, these walls and towers protect us against enemy horsemen. But they are no defense against the unseen arrows of oppressed people, whose moans leap walls and sweep worlds to destruction. Try to acquire the blessings of your subjects -- not only Sunnis, but Shia and Christians, even the Jews. The people are the strongholds, not the turrets."

Nodding his understanding, the sultan asks what brings the Master to the palace.

"Another idea for our safety. As you know, the Mongols are almost here. And it is my duty to protect the Brothers, as it is yours to protect the city. Please send a messenger to the Mongol leader with a gift of those silver-footed bowls that he finds so precious. Tell him Konya will pay a tribute for peace. Any price he asks."

The sultan's brows rise, his turban tilts. "Yes, Master, it is done."

Seven days later, a messenger arrives with a note for Rumi. His hand trembles as he reads, "Sultan Aloeddin Kaykobad has received word: the Khan accepts the bargain. In the name of God, the compassionate and merciful. From the sultan, in whom He has deposited His confidence." Rumi drops the parchment and sighs with relief as tension drains from his body.

The next afternoon, Rumi spends the day mediating a conflict between two families. Now, awaiting the night prayer, he rests on a cushion savoring a quiet moment. A scent of garlic lingers from the evening meal. The rosy light from the oil lamp glows softly. But he is not content. He misses Bahaoddin terribly, the warm, familiar melody of his voice as it reached into the hearts of his followers, the calm certainty in his eyes as they embraced him, his son.

Searching the Koran for solace, he reads, "The pure of heart will be in bliss." *Yes, Father is with God now. The Mongols are staying away. But I am alone and restless. It is time for me to marry.*

Returning the book to its leather pouch on a ceiling hook, he conjures up an image of Gevher, his childhood friend, her round face and round eyes, her thin, round mouth. And his spirits are lifted. But his throat tightens at the same moment, his joy laced with sadness. *If only father were here to perform the marriage.*

Two weeks later, the wedding contract signed, Rumi greets his bride at the large wooden front door. She wears a white eyelet skirt with a long pink scarf with tiny mirrors draping over her shoulders. Her hair is tied back beneath a white scarf, which is trimmed with gold coins and white shells. Her copper-colored skin shines with freshness as she blushes under his gaze.

Lifting Gevher's hand, he places it lightly on his own arm, consummating their first touch. He has been near her, but never this near. He hears her breathing, a small "hsss" as she exhales.

Then quickly the women whisk her away from him, and he is pulled by the Brothers down a corridor, under an archway, and into the reception area, where he links arms with the men and circles to the music of lutes, viols, and drums. Two Brothers lift their legs to imitate a courtship dance of cranes. Three others break off and swing their arms vigorously in imitation of battle.

Leaving them to dance, he moves toward the kitchen and hears Gevher and the other women clapping tambourines and prancing around the hearth fire. After calling out to signal his entry to the women, Rumi wraps his fingers around his wife's and leads her toward their appointed bedroom at the rear of the house.

Gevher lets go of his grip and together they scan the room. Carpets designed with blue, green, and red chevron patterns and hexagons cover the walls. His books fit neatly into a wall niche, and a patched robe and two shirts are folded up in a corner. A ceramic oil lamp painted with flowers hangs from the ceiling. Two yellow rose buds lie on the *kilim*-covered cushions at the head of the sleeping mat. He hopes it pleases her.

Rumi pours water into a metal bowl, bends down, and begins to remove Gevher's shoes. She leans back on her hands and, slowly and gently, he washes her feet, stroking the velvet bottoms and wiggling the toes, so small and delicate. Setting aside the bowl, he joins her on the sleeping mat.

Sitting side by side, he feels awkward and shy. Lifting a finger, he strokes her cheek. "Gevher, may any child from our union be guarded from Satan, God willing."

After scratching his beard, he pulls off his turban, places it upright on the floor, and turns toward her. Her gaze is cast down, her lashes long, her lips moist. She pulls the scarf from her shoulders, its inset mirrors glittering as it moves. The white skirt drapes around her legs. She unties her headscarf and shakes out her hair, as black as a starless night. His young friend, this girl, seems suddenly womanly, as if a wedding contract has changed her already, as if in becoming a wife she also becomes an adult.

As she lifts her head, their eyes meet for an instant, and he seems to lose himself in chestnut-colored waters. But she ruffles and quickly raises the back of her hand to her face, the fingers veiling her. He does not know what to do next.

Stretching out on her back, she seems to be offering an invitation to him. So, he climbs on top and rests on the cushion of her, his weight pushing her hips into the dirt floor. Letting his head

31

drop slowly until his lips set lightly on hers, he inhales. But she giggles uneasily, so he moves his head aside.

"Again, please," she murmurs. This time he pushes his lips onto hers and clings to her mouth hungrily. A warm river of honey floods his body, intoxicating him. With his left hand he lifts her robes and places a palm on her secret region, opening the petals of her flower with his fingers. Then he enters and, in moments, his seed is spilling inside her.

He rolls off, onto his right side, leaving his left arm languishing across her belly. His forehead furrows. *This cannot be what sex is all about. This act cannot be the lust that drives men to Satan.*

A sadness comes upon him then, a loneliness and that restless, nagging longing for more, for something greater than marital love, this false, temporary union.

6

The morning breeze has secrets to tell you –
Don't sleep!

It is Gevher's nature to delight in small tasks. In the soft early light, she slips into a flowered blouse, pulls on a long green skirt, and ties a yellow headscarf as slowly and carefully as she did when dressing for her wedding. She surveys the kitchen and begins to arrange things in an order that suits her. The large iron pot with its ladle belongs on the hearth. The eating bowls and drinking vessels should be grouped together to one side. The buckets and washing basins are placed on the other side, near the door. She turns the worn carpet lengthwise across the room, so that more of the stone floor is covered. Then, satisfied that her kitchen is in order, she picks up a cloth and begins to wipe the dust off each object with care.

When she has finished, she goes outside to the courtyard basin and rinses her husband's white shirts and blue robes and hangs them on a rope to dry. Standing back as they flap in the breeze, she enjoys the whipping sound, not hurrying on to the next task. At her mother's house, the courtyard basin and fountain were covered with pink flowering vines that delighted her each spring. But this courtyard is barren and calls out for beauty, for color. It calls out for her hands.

So, she strolls into the garden behind the *medrasa* to see what plants she can move to the courtyard later in the year. Squatting barefoot in the earth, the dirt pushing into the cracks between her toes, she bows to pull weeds. As the coarse, dry soil runs through her fingers, Gevher sees herself at prayer.

To celebrate the end of her first bitter winter in Rumi's house, Gevher invites three neighbor women to her kitchen to make sweet *halva*. She fills a large copper tray with a mound of flour and a ring of sugar, white as snow. When the others enter, she offers them a bowl and together they roll up their sleeves and wash their hands.

The chatting grows silent as they form a circle around the tray. With one hand on their breasts, the women bow, recite an invocation, and chant *"Huuuu,"* then pause and repeat the sacred chant. Laughing and singing, they plunge their hands into the sugar and knead it until it forms a chewy confection.

After dividing it into sections for her neighbors and bidding them farewell, Gevher performs the sunset prayer. When Rumi arrives, she runs to the door with a piece of *halva* in her fingers, offers it to him proudly, and feels satisfaction as he licks his lips.

Gevher doesn't think about why events happen. Thinking is not her way. Her husband's nature is to ponder and reflect, while hers is to accept. *We are like two strands of white jasmine twining around a single pillar.*

Gevher is pleased that Rumi does not need her to be other than she is. He does not ask her to be more modest, more devout, or a harder worker. As a result, she does not know restlessness. It does not occur to her to cross the frontier of the women's quarter or to serve God in any other way.

With the coming of spring flowers, Gevher awakens with her face beaded with sweat and her belly churning. Her urge to vomit is so strong that she keeps a small tin beside the sleeping mat. One day, she tells a servant to collect swaddling and to hang a Koran over the bed with onion and garlic on a spit.

Eight months later, when the snow is a ghostly blue in the moonlight, Gevher squats in the walnut birth chair, gripping its arms, with her husband by her side. The midwife chants "God is great" again and again, filling the room with verse.

Every few minutes, her body writhes, and she whines quietly until, suddenly, she lets out a shrill scream. And an infant wails with life. Letting out a great sigh, Gevher falls limp in the chair, puddles of fluid gathering beneath her on the floor. The midwife takes the baby, places three sesame seeds on his navel, swaddles him tightly, and ties a blue-bead amulet against the evil eye near his neck.

Standing nearby, Rumi remains silent until he can bear it no longer. He signals for the midwife to leave the room and takes the babe in his arms. Those tiny perfect fingers! Those rosy cheeks and fuzzy head! He tickles the silky soles of the baby's feet, as he slurps and giggles. His son will be named Velad and called, one day, Baha Velad.

Perhaps fatherhood will calm my restlessness. Perhaps I will find paradise here, at home with my family, no different from other men.

He holds up Velad's tiny body toward Mecca and whispers in his right ear, "I witness that there is no God but God, Mohammed is his Messenger." He will teach his son to keep the names of Allah between his teeth.

Taking a deep breath, he knows instantly that his wish will not come true. A wife has not completed him. Neither will a son. He is not one of those men.

Nursing, Gevher feeds her infant son the words of the Prophet along with her milk, hoping they will play in his dreams. She cradles him in one arm as she stirs lentils or pulls weeds, knowing the contentment that only a mother knows.

But one day Rumi stays late at the mosque, and she notices Velad becoming fussy, crying and spitting. She sings to him, rocks him, even feeds him poppy-head water to calm him down. But nothing will satisfy the infant.

When Rumi arrives following sunset prayers and takes the baby into his arms, speaking to him in soft tones, Velad settles down instantly and nods into sleep.

As months pass, Gevher watches as her son crawls about on the reception room floor, where the musty scent of men lingers. Pushing his face into his father's prayer rug, Velad rests a cheek on the scratchy mat. Then one day, as daylight fades and the colors on the carpet dim, she enters the room as he is pushing himself up on his skinny little legs and steadying himself with his arms.

But, instead of attempting a tottering walk as she expects, he begins to turn in circles on one foot, round and round, giggling as his arms flail about until he lands on the floor with a thump. Then he gets up and begins to whirl again.

The following year, Gevher squats again in the walnut chair, clutching its arms. When her second child slips into the world with a wail, his father is away at the prayer lodge, lost in contemplation. When Rumi sees the baby the next day, he strokes his head, names him Aloeddin after the patron sultan of Konya, hands him off to her, and dashes away to the mosque.

Gevher accepts that her husband is preoccupied and focuses her attention to the new infant, who is content to rest in her arms. His deep-set eyes, the color of cinnamon, search hers for food or comfort, and hers return the request with love and a full breast. After nursing she sets him in a cradle along with a list of saints and hangs it from the ceiling hook. When he whimpers, she moves the cradle back and forth until he quiets down. *Aloeddin knows nothing but milk, just as his father knows nothing but God.*

Later that day, when Rumi prepares to leave again, Velad stands at the open doorway with wet cheeks, watching his father step out into the yellow morning light. Even while he collects dung and mixes it with straw for fuel cakes, he is awaiting his father's return. Gevher cannot interest him in food or play. At the appointed hour, after prayers and sermons, she watches as the boy runs across the courtyard and meets Rumi with a yelp at the gate, jumping into his arms.

In contrast, Aloeddin whimpers until the men leave. *He wants me all to himself.* He crawls after her from room to room, drinking in her presence as she folds clean clothes and sets them in wall niches or peels white potatoes and snaps green beans. Then one day he sits upright, raises himself unsteadily on plump legs and, holding onto her skirts, pads beside her in bare feet.

When the men gather in Rumi's reception room, Velad sneaks away from her and cuddles up on a cushion among them, as they stroke their beards and wag their fingers, humming with importance. Velad pulls on the hem of his father's robe until Rumi lifts him and sets him on his bony knees. Bouncing to the rising and falling tones of the men's deep voices, Velad seems happier than when she holds him and tells him stories of the Prophet and saints.

Aloeddin remains by the hearth in the kitchen, enfolded in the scented atmosphere and entranced by the women's chatter. Gevher likes to form lions and camels from sweet dough, heat them in the fire until they brown, and offer them to Aloeddin because he savors each bite.

While most young boys become restless and eager to move out of the women's quarters, Aloeddin resists, as though leaving the tastes and smells of her world is too great a sacrifice. Even the men's games do not entice him.

And so her boys move like two rivers that cross the same landscape but never touch. She thinks of Velad as his father's son, dark, thin, and willowy, just as Rumi was Bahaoddin's likeness. Like his father, Velad has a passion for books and hidden meanings. Aloeddin, her son, is light-skinned and pudgy, with large ears that stick out from the sides of his head. His natural concerns, like hers, are the concrete details of life, the rules of the kitchen and the rules of the law. One river runs deep; the other runs wide. *And where will the waters of life carry them?*

7

*Why are you so enchanted by this world
when a mine of gold lies within you?*

On market day, Velad, now six, is eager to go with his father to the *souk* for the first time. As they cross the threshold into the courtyard, the donkey brays and swishes her tail. Chickens strut about pecking the ground, and Velad chases them away, giggling at their clucking noises and rustling feathers.

A disk of light appears behind the craggy mountaintops as he and his father stroll down the lane toward the city. Sneaking a sideways glance up at his father, he secretly hopes that Rumi is proud of him, not the pride of fools but the pride of a man who knows his son will become a *sheikh* just like him.

At the city square, they enter rows of stalls beneath a vaulted roof. Sunbeams float down, giving the air a golden sheen. From his tiny height, he can see only the hems of caftans and sandals beneath billowing pantaloons. The hubbub of husky voices and the clinking of glass weights as buyers and sellers make trades seems to be above him, out of reach. Velad cranes his neck up, but his view is blocked, his curiosity frustrated.

Just then, Rumi bends down and grabs him under the arms, lifting him up and perching him on his shoulders, where his legs straddle his father's turbaned head. Now he can see the entire *souk*. Such relief! Farmers are arranging their grains and fruits in great piles. Traders from India show off colorful silks and leather goods. Those from China display porcelain, and those from Egypt bring large sacks of sugar. Sheep and camels roam among the stalls. And the scents! Spices and perfumes from exotic places.

"Why do people need that red silk, father? Why do women wear the smell of flowers?"

"Let's not concern ourselves with trivial matters, son. Let's speak of what's important – prayer."

For a moment, Velad's chest sinks with disappointment. He wants to know so much about so many things. But his father continues, "As Sufis, we pray to the God of Abraham, Isaac, and Jacob fives times each day -- a love song at dawn when we don't want to wake up and at night when we would rather sleep. A Muslim is one who submits to His will, not his own desires."

Velad is puzzled. The people with silk and perfume must be submitting to their own desires. "Why do we submit to God's will, father? And what does prayer have to do with it?"

"When the Prophet, blessed be He, ascended from the earth into the garden of essence, he saw the angels moving about. Some stood in rapture before the divine majesty. Others bowed in awe. And others remained lost in full prostration. But they were all merged in divine unity, so the Prophet gave us daily prayers, standing, bowing, and prostrating, so that we share his experience in the garden."

"Is there a quicker way to God than praying?" Velad imagines skipping a step or two on the ascending stair to paradise.

Rumi shakes his turban back and forth between the boy's legs, rocking him. "More prayer."

On cue, the *muezzin* circling the minaret balcony calls out, "Come to the highest realization." All at once, the bustling of the bazaar stops as his father sets him down onto the ground. Women lift tall, reed baskets from their heads. Traders unfurl colorful carpets, kick off their shoes, and face Mecca, bowing and prostrating in unison.

Velad places his hands on his knees, imitating his father beside him, but peeks out to see what others are doing. A clutch of women is making prayers off to one side of the bazaar, their red, orange, and pink backs forming a colorful huddle. Even small children, who have been roughhousing, stop calling each other names at the sound of the *muezzin* and remember the name of Allah. For an instant, his questions subside.

Two Ramadans later, Velad goes with his father from the harem to his first day of school. Bouncing along beside Rumi, he tingles with anticipation. *Finally, I will study the* Shari'a, *the sacred law, with other boys. Finally, I am on my way to becoming a scholar, like father.*

Entering a small room attached to the mosque, they see a large, burly teacher with a hooked nose and a serious manner reclining on *kilim*-covered pillows, while several young boys sit attentively on red and blue carpets at his feet. Rumi squeezes his son's hand and leaves the room.

Velad approaches the teacher and bends his knee, kissing the back of his rough, hairy palm.

"La ilaha ill'Allah means there is no god but God," the teacher is saying. "There is nothing outside of divine unity." He tells Velad and the others that this testimony distinguishes him and all Muslims from the unbelievers. As he takes a seat on a cushion, Velad wonders why the unbelievers do not proclaim this too.

Waving his arm, he asks, "Teacher, why. . . ?"

"Shhhh. Listen without interrupting. Even when events seem incomprehensible to you, or worse, twisted by the hand of the evil one, remember: God is their cause. He is the calligrapher and He is the pen."

Resting on an elbow, Velad tries to imagine a giant man, his towering turban as high as a minaret, who is writing with a giant pen, which stretches the length of his body and extends from it like a finger – because he also *is* the pen. In his confusion, his mind suddenly stops. Shaking his head, he shrugs his shoulders – and simply allows it to be true.

But the teacher sees his bewilderment. "Velad, God is He whom the boldness of thought cannot contain. Your small mind cannot understand, it can only believe."

Then I will try to believe what he teaches me, not figure it out, Velad concludes, nodding.

"Marriage," the teacher continues, "provides a man with children and keeps him from forbidden passions. But it also preoccupies him, distracting him from religious duties with lust and envy."

The other boys squirm about on their cushions. But he feels no restlessness, only eagerness to learn more and more.

"Don't be tempted by the witch of Kabul, who teases you with the colors and perfumes of the world. If you indulge in your desires, even pious acts can't save you," the teacher admonishes. "The devil enters your heart through anger, jealousy, pride, desire for wealth, and lust. You must control them through the sacred law of commandments and prohibitions and through repeating the name of God."

He wags a long finger at the boys. "Turn your soul away from the world, the prison of false gods, and rely on God alone."

Just as contentment begins to descend on Rumi's family, Gevher's wrists and ankles become puffy and sore. Her face swells and she finds it difficult to move about. A doctor diagnoses dropsy, which is causing her tissues to fill with too much fluid.

Lying on her mat, she feels tired and weak when Rumi comes to wish her well. "God desires that people get ill so that He can practice His medicine. You will recover, God willing," he says, kissing her forehead.

But Gevher is uneasy. She sends for two neighbor women and together they design a remedy to add to their prayers. One brings into the courtyard a skinny ram, whose hair is gray and sticky. The other rolls in a cart with four large vats of plant dye from the carpet maker. As Gevher reclines against the door, her neighbors paint the ram's horns gold and its coat red, green, and brown. Finally, they place a blue ribbon around its neck.

One woman holds up the animal's head in her hand while the other draws a long, sharp blade across its neck, shouting "In the name of God." Blood spurts onto their robes and spills onto the courtyard. As Gevher staggers back to her room, they carry the carcass behind the house and carve it into portions for alms.

But the sacrifice does not enable Gevher to raise herself up from the sleeping mat. Day after day, she grows weaker, her breath becoming a faint breeze.

8

Thoughts of the Beloved will feed your soul.
How can your hunger be satisfied
by thoughts of bread alone?

Moving across the courtyard toward his goal, Shams of Tabriz slows down as he approaches a fountain and sees the back of a blue-robed man bending forward over the bowl, his hands behind him, fingers laced together. Passing around the *sheikh*, Shams turns to face him and observes him staring intently into the dark pool, his lips pursed, his forehead furrowed.

The familiar fury rises like a storm in his chest, reaching up to his throat, and thundering out, "What are you doing?"

Holding his focus on the pool, the *sheikh* responds flatly, "I'm watching the moon in this basin."

Shams shoots back, "Why don't you just lift your head to see the moon as it is, instead of in a reflection."

The *sheikh* seems to reel, nearly losing his footing, and turn toward him. His eyes clear as if coming out of a deep sleep. "I recognize the truth of what you say and ask to be your disciple."

"You don't have the strength to bear my company."

"The strength is within me," the *sheik* pleads.

"Then bring me a pitcher of wine, and we will drink together."

The *sheikh* freezes, his head rotating from side to side. "I cannot."

"You see, you are timid, worried about what others think. It is the wine of love that makes us God-intoxicated. I seek only he who knows how to reach the truth." Shams squares his shoulders and exits the courtyard.

For unending years, it has been this way: news of one with a reputation for sanctity, holiness. An arduous journey, a crying out in his heart. Then a meeting – and the realization that once again this is not the one he seeks. Once again, a man who teaches others but knows nothing, who recites formulas but does not reflect, who obeys the ritual of the faith but does not submit. Another empty vessel.

I'm sick and tired of spiritual counterfeits. Those fakirs *who gain fame by walking on hot coals or plunging a knife through their throats do not know* baqa, *God consciousness; they know only magic. Those sober Muslims who claim they alone have a correct understanding do not know* baqa; *they know only past knowledge.*

With resignation, he trudges through the city gates, past grazing goats and bleating sheep, toward his inn, the shade of date palms on the distant horizon.

Long ago in Tabriz, Shams hears tales of saint-like Babas whose charisma is far greater than their scholarly knowledge. One glassy-eyed man in the village can recite no more than the opening verse of the Koran. He does not have a teacher or a spiritual lineage of his own, but the villagers understand that he knows the truth of the holy book. He wanders about in a flowing robe, emitting serenity, compelled by a voice no one else can hear. And he seems to the youthful Shams to give off light.

Shams' family lives in a one-room burrow that is hollowed out of a clay hillside, with earth piled high for walls and a rooftop. Lambs graze nearby on parched grasses and wild hyacinth. A separate storeroom, once used by his mother for making fermented millet, sits empty. The vegetable garden plot is choked with weeds that climb as high as his nine-year-old chest.

One day, as he approaches home, scruffy and tired, Shams hopes for something more than onion and garlic to flavor his bread. Bearing the bruises of another tumble with that pushy Osman, son of a leather tanner, he sidles up to his father, who reclines on their well-worn, cream-colored pillow. The earthenware jar in the center of the room, which holds a mixture of burning straw and dung, no longer radiates heat. The boy sits down, setting his bare feet on the uneven lumps of cold dirt, pulling up his knees to his chest, and becoming still, seeking warmth from the sullen man.

"Father. . ." he hesitates.

The man turns swiftly, reaches for something and -- "thwat!" -- swats him on the back with a conifer branch.

"Father . . ." another smack, this time on the head, his brow throbbing.

Shams tips over onto his side, whimpering and squeezing his eyes shut. His father remote as a stranger again, he pulls into himself, deep into a cave in his own heart. *I don't need him. I don't need anyone at all. But one day, someone, somewhere will know my heart.*

The wish to touch his father's gown has evaporated, and he curls up more tightly on his side in the dirt. At the same time, another part of him remains acutely aware of his father's presence, the man's shifting moods and hasty gestures, the danger of another "thwat!" The air in the house is full of menace.

Today, decades later, he approaches another city and senses that same menace all around him. He has been trained to smell it, and he knows with certainty that it is here, now, in Kaiseri, about to overtake him. His breath shortens, his shoulders tighten, and a cord in his neck bulges.

A black cloud rises from the horizon, and a patch of darkness spreads a contagion across the pale blue canvas above. The acrid odor of ash fills his nostrils. Kaiseri is aflame.

Rows of mud-brick houses are blackened and scorched, their doors singed, their gardens trounced by fleeing families. The shops are burnt shells, their roofs collapsed, their goods looted.

Shams steps into a puddle of blood, and his toes turn crimson. As he lifts his sandal, it sticks to the dirt with a sucking sound. He follows a thin, winding, scarlet river to its source and comes upon a rubble heap, wood and stones and sticks piled high. And then he sees it: a human leg protruding from the heap, its bronze hue reddened, and then a woman's arm, its hennaed hands darkened to black. Trembling, Shams blinks away a tear and stands upright to offer a prayer for the dead. "Allah, forgive them. Give them peace."

But the words do not calm him. He tries again, striving to keep his attention focused, but his supplications do not help. Instead, he clutches at his chest against a cutting pain. Trying to shake off this unfamiliar state, to rouse himself and force his legs, now heavy and numb, to move onward, he wavers and stumbles forward, swaying from side to side.

Everywhere, the streets are littered with bodies: small children curl motionless in women's arms. Men are splayed out, belly to the dirt, caught by a deadly shaft, or face up, pinned to the earth like animals about to be skinned. Whole families stretch around their wells, perhaps hoping the water would save them, their bodies half buried in earth.

Shams cannot breathe. His mind grasps at understanding. This is not the first time Islam is under attack, and it will not be the last. The followers of the Nazarene, those fair-haired knights carrying their cross, assaulted the people of the faith. Now the Mongol infidels are slaughtering believers, attacking the strongholds of those sultans who converted to Islam. The vast empire of the Seljuks, spreading from the Ural mountains to the Persian Gulf and the Indus Valley to the Euphrates, is under siege. Just last month, those dirty nomads left the city of Erzurum in ruins. And now Kaiseri.

In a gesture of faith, his cheeks moist, he lifts his head -- and beholds the needle point of a towering minaret climbing above the rubble. The great mosque and hospital of Kaiseri might still stand, a refuge among the ruins.

He draws near. Columns of gritty smoke rise from the mosque, leaving its right side a hollowed shell. Small fingers of flame leap from the sacred tower, slowly turning it to ash. A solitary *sheikh*, reluctant to leave God's house, lies face down, his robes spreading around him like dark wings, a battered copy of the Koran near his left hand, a single arrow rising out of the center of his back.

Shams stands over him as blood pools, thickening and drying in the heat. *This man clutched his Koran to the end. He could have been a true friend of God.* Shams sighs, his shoulders slumping. *But he was probably another impostor like all the others.*

A scrawny goat wheels back toward a gutted structure. It could be a *jinn*! Perhaps the lost soul of this poor *sheikh* is returning to the world because it is unprepared for paradise.

Shams begins to wonder if anyone is left alive in Kaiseri when a boy dressed in loose-hanging bits of rag, his dirty face clenched like a fist, comes out from behind the mosque. For an instant, the dervish

46

considers moving past him, no reason to stop. But the boy remains motionless, staring, until he extends a small hand slowly, palm up.

Shams has no choice. He must respond, so he moves forward to close the distance between them. Reaching into his robe, he pulls out a thin silver *dirham*, bends forward and drops it into the muddy, outstretched hand.

But the gesture is not enough. Sinking to his knee, he reaches across the boy's shoulder and draws him in, clutching the small bony form fiercely. He feels the child's warm, fast, shallow breath in his ear. *For this moment, no one will hurt you. For this moment, you will be safe.*

The boy wrangles out of Shams' arms and stands back for an instant, his face relaxed, his gaze softened. Then he turns on his heel and dashes away past the crumbling mosque onto the road.

Shams teeters on his feet. It seems that he might fall endlessly into a well of sadness. He goes inside his heart to see how it is. *The whole world is weeping. I am witnessing the collapse of time, the heights of materialism and decadence and the depths of poverty and hunger. Unbelievers thrive, while believers go homeless. Nothing makes sense!*

He has heard what the sober Muslims are saying about the invasions: the faithful are lax in their prayers, lazy in their ablutions, remiss in the pilgrimage. They are permitting innovations, deviating from the true path, even becoming idolaters. For these reasons, God is turning away.

He knows what the Christian monks believe: in public they offer sympathy, but privately they insist that if the Crusaders had won more souls for Christ, if He had washed away their sins, this disaster would not be happening.

Finally, Shams knows that the menace he breathes into his body is death itself. He must lift his feet, step by step toward the friend of God, toward his destiny. He must let himself be pulled forward by Allah, as the moon pulls the tides.

9

Join the company of saints
and know the delight
of your own soul.

A short, slim youth with a round, oily face and sparse beard breathes heavily as he lumbers uphill toward the mosque, his head bowed. At the summit, he is before it, at last. Built of gray stone cubes, it is topped with a single melon-shaped dome. Two needle-thin minarets flank the arched entrance, which is inscribed in blue script: Sultan Aloeddin Kaykobad, January, 1243, God the Forgiver, God the Dominant, God the Bestower, God the Provider, God the Opener, God the All-Knower.

It was built only six months earlier. Sighing with a mix of hope and fear, he kicks off his shoes and steps inside. Massive marble pillars lead up to great arches, which lead up to domed ceilings that are painted with repeating braided floral designs. On red patterned rugs that stretch the length of the hall, dervishes, merchants, traders, and boys, dressed in robes and turbans of many colors, sit cross-legged in crooked rows facing the prayer niche.

Crossing the carpet, its wool smooth and fine beneath his bare feet, the boy sits down in a corner as a tall, dignified man appears and ascends the carved wooden pulpit. Solemn and impeccable, the *sheikh* wears black robes and a white turban. His wheat-colored skin is smooth, his long face and nose accentuated by a scraggly beard still black with youth. *He must be Master Jelaluddin Rumi.*

The *sheikh's* words resonate through the hall, "There is no God but God. Mohammed is His Prophet, blessed be He." Then silence.

The well-worn declaration, which he has heard so many times before, echoes in him for the first time. In childhood he thought they were ordinary words, repeated out of obedience, repeated endlessly until they meant nothing. But today *he* exalted them, arousing him somehow.

Rumi holds a manuscript open in both palms, seeming to feel its weight, then using his left hand to turn the pages gently, ever so gently, as if the parchment might tear – and a life would be lost. He stops, for no apparent reason, and reads aloud a verse, the words tumbling like a waterfall.

"In whatever direction you may turn, there is only the essential face of Allah."

The boy feels irresistibly drawn to Rumi, whose voice seems to beat to the rhythm of his own heart.

Again, the Master holds the book in both palms and gently closes it, speaking to no one in particular but perhaps to hear the ring and rhythm of the words, which he seems to savor like a sweetmeat. "But He is so near that you cannot see Him."

For an instant, Rumi speaks only to him, uttering words that he alone could hear. The other students move about restlessly, their eyes roving the walls. But he sees only the Master, a kind, quiet, inward-looking man who appears somehow remote from those sitting on the hard floor and who seems to stare not at the world but behind it. He appears, in the boy's mind's eye, like a magician who can turn dross into gold.

Suddenly, the aromatic scent that the Master seems to inhale wafts up to him on a breeze that comes through an open window. He no longer hears the words. He is walking through a garden dense with green foliage, the fragrance of apple blossoms in the air.

From far away, he returns to the room with a start. In front of him, the Master still stands at the pulpit, embracing the men with his gaze. He still speaks, each word bursting into the air like a flower. The listener has no clue where he was the moment before.

As he stretches his body, he regards the other students and feels a kinship with them. *At last, I'll be a part of something larger than my own little life. Yes, I want to be a Sufi dervish. I want to obey him and to become Brothers with these men.*

So, after the discourse, he approaches Rumi shyly. "Master, my name is Shahid, and my mother left me here to develop a pious nature. I pray that you will accept me as a student."

Rumi looks down on him from a great height, cocks his head for a moment, and stares through him. Shahid feels exposed. As he squirms with embarrassment, the Master lifts his chin and peers off into space, his lips tightening.

Shahid learns later that when a boy petitions to be a disciple, Rumi looks into his soul. He senses when a boy is ripe, ready to be opened, or when he is dried and hard, only following another's wishes. For a ripe one, he knows when to squeeze and when to pluck. And he senses immediately which *zikhr*, or meditation practice, will best fit his needs. This inner knowledge comes to him swiftly, as a woman knows why her baby wails.

On that day, when Shahid petitions him, Rumi's chin comes down and his attention returns from far away. He nods affirmatively, "*Insh'allah*, if God wills."

Shahid knows nothing about joining a Sufi community. *I might be forced to study, even memorize the Koran. I might be reduced to begging for alms or told to give up sex, like a Christian monk. But, certainly, I won't be alone anymore.*

When he learns that he will be left completely alone in a cell for forty days to pray and fast before being accepted, he is devastated. He thought that he would be at the Master's side like a shadow from that day onward. When Rumi stood before the students to teach Koran, Shahid would sit attentively in the front row on the edge of his seat for hours on end. When Rumi sat lost in prayer for prolonged hours, Shahid would stand off to the side, awaiting his return. When Rumi wandered the hills in springtime, commenting on the early blooms or the newborn lambs, Shahid would nod in agreement.

But no, not yet. First, he must do *halvet*, a solitary retreat, alone with God. . . or without.

He is led away by a stout, dark Arab, who sways like an elephant as he waddles toward the kitchen at the rear of the *medrasa*. Plodding behind him, Shahid enters the room, which is warm and close and smells of rice and rosemary.

The man rotates clumsily to face him. "I am Mehmet, the master of novices. Here you will take the first test of your retreat." He points to a concrete slab covered with a red carpet and sheepskin. "Sit on your knees at the sheepskin post for three days without sleeping or speaking. You may move only to pray, eat one meal after sundown, and relieve yourself with my permission. You will meditate on *'la ilaha ill'Allah,'* there is no God but God, as often as you can.

"If you break the rules of the *halvet*, you'll have to begin again. After three days, you will return to your cell to complete the *halvet*, coming here to work in the kitchen, where both food and men are ripened and cooked." He smirks at his own joke.

Shahid wants to run, to get away as far as possible from this fat, tyrannical man, from the sweltering odors of the kitchen, from the stone-cold floor. He sees himself striding up the hills around Konya, feeling the cool breeze move through his trousers.

Instead, he folds his knees on the pelt, to the left of the kitchen entrance, and tries desperately to get comfortable. Mehmet walks out, leaving him to scan the room. Off to one side, the charcoal brazier gives off warmth. Metal tubs, large and small, sit in crooked piles, their ladles set aside. Pitchers filled with unknown drinks are atop a stone shelf. A brass candlestick is ready for the next ritual occasion.

Shahid squirms. *My mother would be proud of me now, learning to be a devoted Sufi. My mother. . .* His heart aches. Only ten days ago, they wandered away from their mud house in Cappadoccia, in the Eastern portion of the Seljuk Turkish region, leaving behind nothing but an old goat. As they walked, the ground beneath their feet became as soft and white as powdered snow, and the path disappeared among cone-shaped stones that rose from the flat ivory plains to perfect points.

As a boy, he had wondered about the powers of the wind and rain to sculpt the land into those shapes, especially those that stood thick and white at the bottom and rose to a dark cap that fitted like a mushroom top on the base. During those years he had tried to climb and scramble to the peaks, eager to see the view from on high. But the rock had been too smooth to grip his sandals and he never reached a summit. He had never seen what the falcons see as they fly high above the earth.

His mother did not want to travel alone, so they joined a small caravan going south toward Konya, a band of rowdy men with a tired spotted pony carrying rugs and a weaver and his black-shrouded wife in a rickety wooden cart drawn by the family donkey. Frightened of them at first, he kept to himself, treading silently beside his mother across the hills, which were dotted with twining yellow squashes and clumps of brown potatoes. But after three days he became more comfortable with the company, and they roamed with ease through rows of poplars and groves of olive trees, as he picked handfuls of the tiny bitter black fruits and left a trail of pits in his tracks.

They continued wending their way across the dry, rubble plains until the weaver pointed out a great lake made of salt. Soon after, a giant mountain cone came into view. Then the minarets of Konya appeared in the sky in all directions.

He and his mother crossed a moat and proceeded hand in hand in the direction of the mosque on the hill. Part way up the incline, she released his grip and peered down at him, her fingers trembling as she touched his cheek. Kneeling, she set a bundle on the ground and unwrapped it quickly, pulling out a well-worn copy of the Koran. She handed him the sacred book as she rose up.

"Son, I pray that, in time, you will reveal a pious nature and that your studies will make a mother proud." Rotating on her heel, she fled down the hill, her black gown swinging from side to side, her bundle tucked under her right arm.

Yes, she would be proud of me now. Fasting and meditating. . . oh, I forgot, "There is no God . . . ."

An aching sensation in his loins breaks his reverie, but he forces his attention back onto his knees, which press against the hard surface. His penis throbs, and his right hand reaches down to soothe it. "There is. . . ." He feels the familiar snake form fill out beneath his grasp. *The demons are tempting me already!*

He yanks his attention back to the *zikhr* and begins to chant the sacred words, "There is no God but God. . . There is no God but God. . . There is no God. . ." But his mind will not be still. It leaps from thought to thought like a buzzing bee from flower to flower, each one holding the promise of sweet nectar.

I will finally become a religious man, a Sufi on the path to holiness. Pride appears at the center of that flower.

Surely, I will never achieve as high a spiritual station as Rumi, who must have conquered his demons. Envy appears at the center of that flower.

I am scared to move, but no one will ever know. He extends his stiff legs, as cheating appears at the center of that flower.

Exhausted after only a few minutes of this inner battle, Shahid gives up and lets go. His head falls forward and he drifts into sleep, dreaming that he fails the retreat and is taken to the city gates, cast out of the community.

Awakening with a start, he gasps for air. Smoke wafts up, enveloping him in the scent of rosemary. *I am still where I am supposed to be, at the kitchen post. I still have a chance to belong.*

The hunger pangs do not let up. His mouth is parched. His bowels expel fetid air. A dull headache hangs over his right ear and slowly spreads across his forehead until it feels like a heavy woolen cloth lies on his skull, numbing his mind. It throbs, and he cannot recite one more prayer.

10

Every vision born of earth is fleeting;
Every vision born of heaven is a blessing.

Whether he is praying, reading, or teaching, Rumi is fighting off a sense of foreboding. *God would not let Gevher die. The children need their mother until they become men. God would not. . .*

The fear compels him to go see her, to feel reassured in her presence. But Gevher's round face is as swollen as a splotched, overripe peach. Her arms, resting on a blanket, bulge like full udders. Her youth, her beauty have passed in a moment, as fleeting as a flower petal. *This earth eats us. It devours us all at once.*

Stroking Gevher's head, he tries to soothe her. "Have faith, Gevher. This disease, this excess of fluid, is the insatiable thirst for the water of life."

She grunts and takes his hand in hers. But her palm is too small and swollen to cup his long, bony fingers in their entirety. Gently, he reverses the hold, taking her puffy palm into his knuckley grip. He raises it slowly to his lips and gently kisses the center of her open hand, then sets it back on her heart.

The crescent moon, a white sail, hangs in the blackness, bringing Ramadan around again. Aloeddin was looking forward to his first fast and to celebrating the Night of Power at its conclusion, when God's revelation of the Koran descended to the Prophet, blessed be he. His mother told him to place the hunger in his soul, and it would make unpleasant things pleasant. So, he hoped he would be able to master his craving for food.

But now, on his haunches on the sleeping mat, Ramadan is only beginning and already he feels spent. He is furious at God, at His lack of justice, at His lack of caring. *God is letting Mother die. Why obey a God like that?*

Dashing out into the streets, Aloeddin shakes his fists at the air, railing at Allah, "How can you let my mother suffer so? What kind of God are you?" until, his face flushed, he crumples to the ground in a heap.

By the third day, the hunger gnaws at him. After the noon prayer, he sneaks into the kitchen and sees a lone date on a tray. Without warning, the fruit's sugary taste fills his mouth. *What if. . .*he tries to chase away the forbidden thought. But it steals back. *What if I ate when it was forbidden?* His stomach twists into a knot. He approaches the date, circles it, and marches off again, out of the kitchen. *I cannot violate the fast!*

Why not? God doesn't care about me! Why should I care about God?

Defiant, he sneaks back, grabs the dried fruit, and hides it under his cloak. His belly gurgling, he licks his lips, wondering, if he bites into it, whether his father will find out. Whether he will lose a chance at paradise for all time.

He glances about. No one sees him there. He rips off a piece of date and sets it on his tongue. As it moistens and crumbles, he waits. No sign that God sees him either.

He jams the other half into his mouth, pure sweetness. Holding his breath, his jaw tightens. No one notices.

Twice he disobeyed God's law – and twice he got away with it. He raises his head upward and cries, "We're even!"

The new moon brings the end of the fast, but Aloeddin cannot look forward to the feast. Other boys and men move up and down the streets carrying sheep on their shoulders or dragging them by their horns to the sacrifice. At Mecca, 120,000 animals will be killed, the roads running with blood in celebration.

But Aloeddin is too distraught to care. His mother remains in a back room, wrapped in rugs, her head curled into her chest. Brown circles outline her eyes, her belly is distended, her legs bulge with fluid. She lies unmoving on the mat from dawn to dusk, her breathing labored, her stare glassy and remote.

Each morning, he brings her hot tea, but the glass remains full. Each evening, he feeds the blaze in the hearth and leaves wood for her to maintain it, but the woodpile is untouched, the blaze becomes embers.

One afternoon, she calls him to her side. "Aloeddin, go and collect kindling for the fires. Tell Velad to take a bowl of bean soup to Kabir down the road, who is ill with the fever."

Then, as he watches, she rises from her mat, telling him she intends to end her idle days. And his faith rises too. *Mother, in the kitchen, cooking again.*

But while swamping a pot of rice with clarified butter, she collapses, and he staggers up to catch her as she hits the floor. "Mother, Mother, don't leave me. Please don't leave me," he begs.

Heavy in his arms, she reaches up and lightly touches his cheek. "Your mother loves you, son. Have faith and obey Allah always." Then she falls back and slips away from him.

"Noooo!" howls out of his mouth.

Releasing her to the floor, he tries to collect himself and to reason. *God is merciful and compassionate. He would not take Mother too soon. She is a pious Muslim who obeys His law.*

Rising up, he darts past the reception room and through the door. Outside, the light shines jagged through the trees. He races out of the courtyard into the lane, trying to calm his mind, but thoughts bombard him. *Mother said, if you love Allah, He will love you. If anyone loves Allah, it is mother. And yet God has taken her measure and found her wanting. Why? Why?*

Maybe God is asleep. Maybe He is napping today. Or maybe He fails to remember her obedience. Does God forget?

Aloeddin shakes his head. Such a disaster cannot be God's fault. Mother. . . maybe she is being punished for some forbidden act. Maybe she secretly ate swine or breathed swear words in a flash of anger.

Aloeddin's gut churns. *No, it is my fault.*

He tries to bury the thought, stuff it down into darkness – but sweet date lingers on his tongue. He stops in his tracks. He has not broken the fast without consequences after all. God does watch over him.

Falling to his knees on the hard dirt, he pleads, "Allah, forgive me. Please, forgive me."

Suddenly, in his imagination a huge *sheikh* in a white river of robes emerges, his face as big as the moon and as wrinkled as a leather pouch. But he is forbidden to see God's face! It is only permitted to believers after they die.

Like his mother. Maybe now she can look on God's face.

"Please, Allah, let her walk in your garden and see you face to face. I will never break the sacred law again. I promise."

From behind the house Rumi hears his son's wail shatter the silence. When he rushes in, a sour stench greets him. Gevher is on the kitchen floor, her robes fallen around her in a heap, her brow beaded with sweat, her hair forming a halo on the stone.

He steps closer. Her face is a gray mask. Her robe and shoes seem mask-like too, the life spilled out of them already. He touches her hair, feathers in his hand, and places his forehead on the hard, cold ground.

That night Gevher appears in his dream, a frail girl standing beside her father so long ago, while Sufi travelers load horses and carts to prepare for exile from Balkh. Smiling, she is eager to let him know she will be joining him in the caravan, she will join her life to his wherever they go. And she tells him without words, just that smile.

Alert in the darkness, alone on the mat, the familiar sound of his wife's breath hisses beside him. *Perhaps the veil between the living and the dead has been torn away.* Then silence.

Later that night, under a black shroud, Rumi awakens weeping, "Gevher, Gevher," sobbing his grief in her name, his *zikhr*.

For forty days, streams of people enter and leave the sitting room while recitations of the Koran go on and on. The women keen inconsolably, spreading dirt on their heads. The men rip their shirts, and the mourning period seems endless.

But the memory of Gevher's smile carries Rumi through the grief. Without it, the weight of the loss could have dragged him to earth, burying him with her. But that shy smile – its innocence, its promise – reveals their years together in one sweet moment.

When Rumi's father died, he believed he lost the milk of life. When his wife died, he lost the honey. Yet somehow he knows that she was not the source of honey. *The wish for fulfillment through family life is deceptive. The pain in my chest is the result of loving someone, anyone other than God.*

11

God's creation is vast –
Why do you sit all day in a tiny prison?

On the fourth day of the *halvet*, Shahid can barely stay awake. When Mehmet appears at the kitchen door, his words seem to come from far away.

"Shahid, it's time for the ritual bath. Come now."

After washing three times, Shahid receives the garment he will wear for the remainder of the retreat and slips it over his head. Then Mehmet reaches into the folds of his wide, hanging gowns and hands him a soft cap of white wool, which tapers toward a point.

"Here's your *elifi*. It's named for the first Arabic letter because they share the same shape. You'll need to wear it during communal prayer and *zikhr* practice. It signifies that you are becoming a part of the Order."

Together they make their way back to the small cell where Shahid will stay for the next forty days. As Mehmet's meaty hand pushes open the door, Shahid's heart sinks. It is cold, dark, and nearly empty. A sleeping mat is rolled up in the corner. A Koran lies on top. The only welcome sign is a pitcher of water and a plate of bread, dates, and olives to break his fast.

"Old Ibrahim awakens us before dawn prayer," Mehmet says. "We have a small meal together, then practice *zikhr* for two hours. The Master says, '*Zikhr* polishes the heart. When it is polished, it will reflect only Him.'"

As he sways toward the threshold, Mehmet slows and cranes his neck back at him. "If you are judged unqualified to become a lover of God, you will find your shoes turned outward at the door. At that time, please leave the seminary at first light."

Shahid shudders. *I only wanted to be near him, to belong. But I am alone, as always.* He removes his shoes, plops down on the cold floor, and wonders what will become of him.

At dawn, a pounding on the door startles him out of a foggy sleep. Ibrahim does not wait to be greeted. His sandals flap on the floor as he steps on to the next cell.

The newborn light slides through the crack. Shahid stretches and moves mechanically through his ablutions and prayers, hoping that breakfast might awaken him to the day. He enters a room beside the kitchen, where dervishes are seated in silence around a long tray.

The cook grabs his sleeve and signals with a nod to come toward him. "As a novice, you will serve your Brothers," he says, handing him a brass urn of hot tea. Shahid places it on the table and re-enters the kitchen, where a bronze bowl of fresh yogurt is placed in his arms. Next, he receives a dish of dates for one hand and a plate of bread for the other. He sets them down and goes back to the kitchen. This time the cook returns with him to the table, sits at one end, and indicates a place for Shahid to sit.

"*Bismillah,* in the name of God," the cook blesses the meal.

Each Brother picks up a spoon, which is laid face down on the table, and scoops yogurt out of the common bowl, then passes it to the brother on his right. Shahid mimics them, but he is barely able to contain his hunger as the bowl goes around the silent circle. Picking up another date, he savors its sweetness on his tongue.

One dervish after another pushes away from the table, and the breakfast is cleared. The Brothers grab the two sides of the tabletop, carry it outdoors, and shake it clean. Shahid ambles back to his cell alone.

As the sun, a lonely traveler, wanders across the heavens, Shahid sits enclosed in darkness, a kernel within its shell. He tries to convince himself that if he will just sit still long enough, if he will just purify his nasty demons, the Master will come and deem him worthy to be a dervish, worthy to belong.

He recalls the caves near his home in Cappadoccia, those misshapen holes dug into the chalky rock, where Christian monks passed years of mortification, sitting like rows of vultures perched with their winged robes tucked beneath them. Someone told him that those monks, following Christ's orders, believed that wrestling with demons could be completed in one rite, rather than requiring a lifelong struggle. Their priests could burn incense and lure the evil spirit out of the body, like a fisherman hooking a carp.

Shahid sighs, wishing it were that simple. *I am not worthy. I will probably have to fight my adversaries -- pride, anger, and envy – for years to come.* And so he tries again to be vigilant, then rests his watch for a while, wakes up, and tries again.

His task is simply to turn inward and remember God. But everything is a distraction to his concentration, yanking his attention this way and that: the pounding noise of Brothers beating carpets, the coughing and spitting of the novice in the next cell, the patting footsteps of the *muezzin* on his way to the minaret before each call to prayer.

And his mind – it never rests, even for a moment. It wanders here and there like a *fakir* through strange lands. His throat is as empty as a hollow flute. He recalls the sweet, moist feel of honey water washing his mouth, soothing his parched lips and sliding down his throat in a cool river. *Oh, to drink one mouthful of honey water, I would do anything.*

Unthinkingly he moves his cold right hand to his belly, no longer a soft mound of flesh but a recess between two rocky hips. A small beast resides there growling. It has not been fed since last evening, but first it will be time for evening prayers. Again, prayers. Welcome only as a signal that food will arrive soon.

Food -- rice noodles with fresh hot lamb pieces, dried fruit with newly curdled yogurt, and *halva*, which melts sweetly and slowly on the tongue. Perhaps a sip or two of grape wine, as his mother used to sneak to him.

No, none of it. Instead, the meal will be a small bit of rice, no meat, perhaps a turnip, a few dates or olives. Certainly, no wine. It will taste of nothing, air in the mouth. But it will appease that small beast whose jaws lie open, waiting.

Shahid's right hand feels a bit warmer now, and he begins to rub his belly, enjoying the feel of the cloth on the skin beneath. The fleshy stem between his legs moves lazily and he startles. He has not felt aroused for many days. The promise of pleasure brings a grin to his face, and he moves his hand down, slipping it beneath the folds, and grabbing hold of his member, shrunken like an empty sleeve but swelling quickly as his fingers run down it.

Warring thoughts force their way in: *I must not do it. I mustn't break the rules of the* halvet. *I have a chance now for a new life, a pious life. I mustn't let the demons control me.*

But no one will know. I'm alone in the cell. I could do it once, just this once.

As he strokes his member again, shivers run up his spine. He lies back on the hard sheepskin-covered post and pulls and stretches it urgently. Just then, the *muezzin*, atop the minaret, looking down on the people of Konya, calls them to evening prayer. Shahid can hear, "Come to the highest realization. . . ."

But he doesn't even glance aside at his prayer rug. He is riding the ocean waves that he heard about as a boy, their rising and falling motions carrying him further and further out to sea. Riding until he bursts, and foam sprays onto his fingers.

His breathing begins to slow down, he drifts. But the patter of footsteps coming closer startles him up into a sitting position. Caught -- a trapped animal. The footsteps pass. Whoever it is wants nothing of him.

Perhaps, after the retreat is over and he receives the frock of the dervish, they will want something of him. They will want. . . *but what do I have to give? A boy with no parents, no trade, and no. . .self-control.*

For his kitchen service, Shahid fetches water, scrubs pots from the evening meal, and sweeps the floor again. His mind is dulled by the routine, and his long skirt is gritty from wiping off his hands on it. But Mehmet has not finished testing his patience and obedience. Now, the cook needs candles for an upcoming ceremony.

"You must buy them from a dervish brother," Mehmet instructs him, "even though there is another candle maker nearby." The master of novices hands him a woven carpetbag that hangs from the shoulder for carrying the tapers back to the seminary.

Shahid steps out onto the streets for the first time in weeks. He moves through a labyrinth of narrow alleys, edged on both sides with high walls. Men stoop in doorways or lead donkeys toward the center of town. Children scamper about. The sounds strike him as louder and harsher than before, seeming to pierce his skin.

From behind a wall he hears women's voices, a harem enclosed in a garden, the perfume of orange blossoms wafting toward him. The scent makes him dizzy, weak in the legs.

He enters a sunlit square, and a regal governor to the sultan rides toward him on a gray pony, its mane neatly trimmed and its tail up in the air. The rider, dressed in a brown coat with gold buttons running down the front and a gold buckled belt, has long, wavy hair, smooth olive skin, and a finely trimmed beard. He swings one leg over the beast's back. A dagger, sheathed in green with a gold handle, rests across his lap. His hands, covered in elbow-high gloves, hold a long stick with black feathers on one end. His feet, covered in soft leather boots, hang off a blue blanket lying across the beast.

Shahid has never seen such a man, such poise, wealth, and power. *Here is someone who values the visible world, not the invisible one. Here is someone who is paid a great number of* dinars, *who is not dependent on the donations of others.*

The novice scans his own frock; it is frayed and dusty. He lifts his cap and runs his hand through his hair. He sees himself through this great man's eyes, his broad hooked nose, oily face, and sparse beard, and he sees pity there. This man thanks God that his own son is not in such circumstances. And what if he knew that this so-called Sufi is a fake, deserving neither pity nor charity?

Shahid desperately wants to hide. He spins about and scampers off, heading into a cool, damp alley, running until he comes back onto the main road, out of breath. In front of him is a candle shop. It is not the one to which he has been sent but, if it has the right candles, Mehmet will never know the difference. He steps inside, where small shelves hold row after row of tapers in all sizes and shapes.

"Asalaam," the shop owner greets him, pouring a glass of hot tea and trying to get him to sit among the cushions.

But Shahid is in a hurry. He drains the tea and, after a moment's hesitation, chooses those candles that fit Mehmet's description. Thanking the shop owner, he runs back through town, places the candles on the kitchen bench, and returns to his cell, where he begins to feel a growing sense of unease about what he has done.

A few minutes later, Mehmet knocks loudly and enters the retreat cell. His patched robe sags over his bulky frame. "A dervish brother followed you in your reentry into the world. You disobeyed my request. Come with me, take your punishment."

Terrified, Shahid walks behind Mehmet out to the courtyard. "You don't deserve to wear the hat of the dervish." The master of novices reaches out his hand to him, and he reluctantly removes his cap and hands it over.

"Now, lift your robes." Before Shahid knows what to expect, Mehmet slaps his legs behind the knees three times with a willow stick, stinging him badly.

"Do you wish to begin the retreat again, or do you wish to leave?"

An image flickers across his mind: he is wandering aimlessly down an empty road, cold and hungry, with nothing but an alms bowl. "Again, please," he mutters.

"This time you will learn obedience, *insh'allah*, God willing."

Forty days later, having swept the floors and cleaned the latrines as often as he polished his heart with *zikhr*, Shahid knows that the retreat is coming to an end. He longs to join the other dervishes but still doubts his worthiness and his ability to obey. And, during prayers and chanting, he still dreams of life outside the seminary and questions whether he belongs here at all. But his devotion to Rumi has bloomed and its sweetness has carried him through the retreat.

That morning, someone is outside his door, and he can hear him melodically reciting prayers. "He alone is First and Last, Manifest and Hidden, Immanent and Transcendent. May this Brother's prayers be accepted by Him."

The man knocks, Shahid opens. And the *halvet* is unsealed.

It is Mehmet, who lowers his weighty body clumsily to the floor and kisses the back of Shahid's hand, then touches it to his own forehead. Shahid freezes: *I don't deserve this honor.*

But in the next instant he rejects that idea. He can no longer indulge in such self-doubt because Mehmet has accepted him. The

Master has accepted him. To doubt his own ability now is to doubt Rumi's judgment.

Mehmet grabs him by the arms, embracing him for a moment. Shahid squirms away when he feels the massive folds of flesh against his chest. Next, Mehmet is stroking his gown from top to bottom, then his own gown, to partake in the blessing that has accrued to Shahid during the retreat.

I need to prove myself to Mehmet now, to prove my ability, no, my loyalty. For this man believes in me.

"Little brother," Mehmet says in a more friendly tone, "you may think you have made a great sacrifice, but the real *halvet* begins after the *halvet*. Come with me."

Shahid follows him into the kitchen, where Mehmet picks up a sharp knife, grabs his chin and cuts a wisp of hair from his beard, then snips a curl from his scalp. Caught by surprise, Shahid opens his mouth to ask what this is about. But Mehmet is already explaining that the ritual demonstrates the rejection of the lower self.

In the next moment, the master of novices places a new flat cap on his head, and Shahid shivers. This is the moment he has anticipated. It is the moment he has dreaded-- his initiation into the dervish brotherhood.

Mehmet indicates to him to be seated on the kitchen floor, sits down opposite him, and begins to describe the *adab* of the order, the rules of conduct that are required for membership. "Shahid, you must not leave your *sheikh* before the eye of the heart opens. You must behave ethically toward others, giving them your service. In our Order, we don't beg for alms, so you must work for your livelihood. You must study hard and, in time, you will marry, like all Muslim men. You must provide hospitality to visiting Brothers and, when traveling, pay your respects to the local *sheikhs*. Do you agree to uphold these rules?"

"I agree." Shahid swallows hard, wondering if he can keep this agreement, and returns to his cell.

After evening prayers, the Brothers gather in the prayer lodge on red and blue carpets around the edges of the room. Shafts of sunlight fall onto the wooden floor.

Rumi enters the hall, striding slowly to his post, his robes swaying. He signals Shahid to come forward. The new Brother kneels, brushes his lips against the back of the Master's hand, and takes the oath of allegiance to the order.

Rumi tells him, "Those who swear allegiance to us are swearing allegiance to God. The hand of God is over their hands."

The Master presents him with the *khirqa,* the cloak of a dervish. As the patched blue robe settles on his shoulders, a confused sadness settles on him too. *Someone has made a mistake. A boy like me cannot serve so wise a* sheikh. *Mehmet must know I am unworthy. Rumi must have seen into me, my ignorance, my passions.*

Or, maybe I am wrong. If they believe I am worthy, maybe I am. If God has chosen Rumi as His instrument, then I will pray to serve him well. And perhaps, through my devotion to him, I can tame my demons.

Rumi continues to address him. "Today Mehmet taught you the outer rules of conduct. Now you will learn the inner rules, the secret *adab.* Behavior that is proper but empty of attention to God is meaningless.

"While you behave honestly, strive to match your actions to your hidden intentions. While you are hospitable, keep solitude and remain detached from worldy things. While you serve the needy, cultivate a soft spot in your heart for compassion. While you practice *zikhr,* remember God and forget your lower self. If you fulfill the law without awareness, it has no value in the sight of God."

Shahid's head is spinning. He knows that wisdom is being passed to him, but he is overwhelmed and cannot take it in.

"And the divine name for your *zikhr* is *al-Ghafir,* God the Forgiver, to ease your fear of your sins."

My sins! Does he see into me after all then?

"Do you agree?" he hears the Master ask from a distance.

"I agree," he manages to mutter.

In the dining hall, the cook serves a special sherbet in his honor. It is icy and tart with the taste of lemons. The tables are set with the brass candelabra from the kitchen – and the white candles, which he purchased himself, are lit.

12

Since the rose is not eternal,
why be captured by its scent?

Night after night, the mat where Gevher slept lies vacant, her *kilim* pillow bare. Rumi leans back against the wall, his turban neglected beside him. He cannot comprehend how life can continue as before.

Toward morning, he strays into the reception room, where the pedestal candle remains unlit, and curls up in a corner. When the basket maker's wife arrives to help with the cooking, he does not greet her. He can hear Mehmet and Iqbal working in the vegetable garden, pounding the soil, but he does not feel grateful to the Brothers.

He wanders back into the bedroom, listless, and spots the <u>Divine Sciences</u> in the wall niche, opening it at random. "Everything in creation is a mother. Mineral, plant, or animal, they all suffer birth pangs in order to produce something higher, something beyond themselves."

Rumi stirs as he begins to glimpse the hidden meaning of the teaching. But just then Aloeddin, his cheeks moist, his nose running, totters into the room. *He's like a flower closing with the loss of daylight. He needs his mother. Nothing else in creation can mother him.*

Aloeddin tilts his head as if he's listening to someone. But no one is there. "Son, what do you hear?"

"Mother is telling me a story. But I can't see her, Father. I can't see her face anymore."

Rumi watches, his heart aching, as the boy roams out of the room toward the kitchen. A moment later, Velad approaches and sidles up to him, wanting to know about paradise, where his mother has gone and whether his father will go there soon too.

Twisting the hairs of his beard between his thumb and finger, Rumi stares down at him. Without a word, he gets up and storms out of the house, letting the door slam shut behind him.

Left crouching in the shadows, Velad whimpers. He must pray and talk to God like his father does. *I promise you, Allah, I will be good so that father will love me and not go to paradise too.*

He pauses, trying to imagine what God wants of him. *At all times, in all circumstances, I will listen and obey my father.*

On his sleeping mat under a dome of darkness, Rumi is gripped by discontent. Stray dogs bark and howl outside. Reaching out his hand as if Gevher were there, only a phantom returns his touch.

After the night prayer, he goes to visit her grave, rests on his haunches, and places his head in the dirt beneath a tall, pointed cypress. "Allah, please forgive her. Don't withhold from her the reward of faith." But the ache in his chest remains.

When the moon slips into the blackness and disappears entirely from view, he hears children on the rooftops pounding drums to call her back to new life, pounding drums to invite the setting moon to rise again. *The setting moon – Gevher is like that. She has disappeared into the blackness but is not gone. She will go down and come up on the other side with a crescent smile.*

13

Oh, the many objects of desire,
the many reflections of His beautiful face.

Rumi decides to bring a man into the house to help with the chores. Tall and slim, with a square chin and sunken cheeks, Sepahsalar arrived from Bursa with a letter of introduction from a Sufi *sheikh*. Dressed in loose brown trousers and a long, blue vest, he begins to take up Gevher's duties in the kitchen and garden.

A full lunar cycle after the mourning period, Rumi tells Sepahsalar that he is thinking about finding another wife who can bring warmth and affection to the boys. A woman who is capable and devoted, intelligent and obedient. But he has no idea where to find such a woman.

That afternoon Sepahsalar comes back from the bazaar and greets him, "Master, a woman named Kira Khatun, the widow of King Nur'aldin, asked me to give you her greetings. Do you know of her?"

"I have heard of her aid to the poor. But tell me what you know of her, Sepahsalar."

"She was a pious, educated Christian woman, known in her quarter as a second Mary. She converted in order to wed a sultan and wishes to remarry in our faith."

"Please invite her to the house after sunset prayers, Sepahsalar."

Hours later, as dusk falls over Konya, Rumi lights the copper oil lamps. One by one, they form small rings of light. Holding the pages of Ibn 'Arabi's book in his lap, he tries to study. The philosopher proposes that the imaginal world exists between the sensory world of forms and the formless spiritual world. When the faculty of imagination clothes spiritual realities in images, they are there and not there, like reflections on polished metal.

But his mind flits about, a restless wanderer. Now he is no longer certain that he wants to meet another woman. He does not know why he extended this invitation so soon. His stomach queasy, he refolds his legs and stretches them out again. He takes a deep breath and tries to concentrate on the book. Imaginal images also appear in dreams, the philosopher says, which are both there and not there. In order to make meaning from them, an interpreter must, like Joseph, mediate between his own imagination and the dreamer's.

Just then, someone knocks. He hesitates, closes the book, and gets up to open the door. Kira Khatun waits at the threshold dressed in a pale blue robe and headscarf, her lips parting, her cypress-green eyes meeting his. Stunned at her beauty and the directness of her gaze, he stares for a moment, then rouses himself and shows her into the room with a sweeping gesture.

When he turns about to face her again, she does not become nervous but remains patient, arms at her sides, and peers back at him unlike Gevher, who always avoided his eyes. He admires her long face with high cheeks, thin brows, and green eyes. His attention is drawn to a strand of straw-colored hair slipping beneath her headscarf. And she gives off a familiar scent, which he struggles to identify. Bread! Kira smells of freshly baked bread.

He cannot stop staring. The room seems suddenly warm and closed in. His skin prickles, and he shifts his weight from side to side to get his bearings.

He imagines what Kira sees as she studies him, his face illuminated in the oil lamp: his coal-black beard and heavy brows, his dark eyes, strong nose, and generous mouth, his high turban and long robes, which hang from broad shoulders. She waits for him to speak.

"*Asalaam alaykum*, Kira Khatun."

"And peace on you, Master."

Beneath the placid words he feels a torrent rushing between them. Heat moves from the center of his body outward like a flash fire until it reaches his skin and burns. His desire shocks him and he casts his eyes down, gluing them to the carpet's woven pattern of flowers and leaves.

Relieved for a moment, he looks up and his eyes land on a wisp of sand-colored hair at the edge of her scarf. *What is this heat -- not the gentle desire I felt for Gevher. More like dry brush catching flame. Father said demon lust is like the teeth and claws of our animal ancestors. If it is not transcended, it will grow to become a dragon. I must avoid its stranglehold by summoning my concentration.*

"I understand you have a daughter?" He swallows hard and looks away as he shows her to a cushion, then sits down opposite her.

"Yes, Master," she says as she takes a seat. "I adopted Kimiya fives years ago when her parents died of the fevers. She is the age of your son, Alocddin." But her brow furrows and her head tilts to the side.

"You have a question, Kira?"

She grins widely, seeming to appreciate his perceptiveness. "Yes, I have been wondering about pain, pain of the heart, especially. What is its purpose?"

Rumi sits back, breathing easier, as he occupies the more familiar ground of teaching. "Pain is our guide in everything. Until you ache for something, you won't strive to attain it. No doubt you know the story of Mary, mother of Jesus, whom we call the Prophet Isa. Wasn't it the pain of childbirth that brought Mary to the withered date tree, which became fruitful? The body is like Mary. Every one of us has a Jesus inside, but until the ache grows in us He is not born."

Kira nods in recognition, and they sit quietly as dusk settles around them.

On the following Sunday, their wedding day, the wheat grass dances on the plains behind Konya, and feathery clouds turn suddenly pink, brushing the sky with the color of roses. When the last guest leaves, Rumi silently pushes the bedroom door ajar. His breath catches at the sight of the long curve of Kira's back. She lets her robe slip off one shoulder, then the other, baring the round mounds of her breasts, the long, shapely arms and thin wrists. With one hand she holds the heavy folds of blue fabric at her hip. With the other she wipes her neck and face.

As she wraps herself in a gauzy white gown, the blue robes fall around her ankles. She steps out of the heap and moves forward, away from him.

Then, reaching up with both hands, she unties the headscarf. He gasps. She spins about, lowering her arms, as the straw-colored hair tumbles down in waves caressing her shoulders. Mesmerized, he stares not at her face but at the golden waves of hair.

He feels a bulge beneath his prickly wool robes, and the intensity of his arousal brings him shame, so he avoids her eyes. As he inhales her scent, he studies the line of her jaw, so fine and clear-cut. Her ear, a delicate labyrinth.

With one more step, he is before her, his hands impatient, grasping at the curls that fall around her shoulders and getting lost in the tangles. His fingers run down her long neck and strong collarbone and grip her round, full breasts. Sinking to his knees on the carpet, he presses his cheek into the slope of her belly, silky and warm beneath the thin cotton gown. She reaches over and puts out the oil lamp.

Before the dawn prayer, Rumi hears Kira slip away to the bathhouse to do a full ablution. Awakening to a wet spot on the mat, he is disturbed. Head in hands, he beseeches God to forgive him. His animal energies roared to the surface, and he desired her lips, her breasts, her sex. And he desires more of her, more than he ever wanted of anyone.

For the first time, he knows the struggles of other men with the demon lust. Perhaps he is an ordinary man after all.

It is like someone broke into my peaceful garden and planted thorn bushes. I feel trapped there, frightened that I will end up running in circles among the thorns, searching for the wrong thing. I could become so hungry for union with my wife that I will no longer thirst for union with God.

He sits upright, folds his legs, and allows his lids to close. As the rocky waves of agitation on the surface of his mind even out, he is drawn inward, toward an ocean of silence. He remembers again who he is. He remembers God's grace and his yearning for Him. *Might my desire for Kira carry a hidden meaning?*

14

This longing,
too large for heaven and earth,
fits easily in my heart,
*   smaller than the eye of a needle.*

His father's death, Gevher's death, now this, the hidden meaning of sex. *I must teach the Brothers the secret I have uncovered.*

After the community performs noon prayers, the dervishes gather around him in the lodge. Some press forward toward the pulpit with eagerness, as though his nearness is precious to them. Others hold back, seeming wary or intimidated. None of them sees him as he is, rather than as he appears.

Emir Pervane sits erect in the place of his prayer. "Do you have questions in your heart, Emir?"

He nods. "Yes, Master, it seems that there are a hundred thousand different wild beasts in man. The beasts in the Mongols want silver saddles and golden bowls. The beasts in my wife want to talk, constant chatter. I desire only to see you, Master, but the business with the Mongols keeps me away. How do we tame these beasts of desire?"

Praise God, He has ordained that the Emir provide me with the ideal question for my teaching.

"Pervane, one man is preoccupied with women, another with wealth, and another with knowledge. Another desires only to see the Master. But each of these is a veil. You do not see me, now, at this moment without a veil. And so it is with desires for every thing – father, mother, heaven, palaces, food. All things are veils.

"In reality, all that we desire is a single thing. 'I want noodles.' 'I want *halva*.' 'I want dates.' But the root of the matter is hunger.

"In the same way, our hunger for people or knowledge is a single thing: All desire is the desire for God."

Yes, my nostalgia for my father, lust for my wife, even the thirst for knowledge, it's all a veil over my yearning for Him. And the Brothers, they are like children with childlike desires, concerned with meeting their own needs, with consuming melons, meat, and sugar. They do not see that these are all just colored dust.

"But the desire for a woman has a purpose, Master -- to make children," Pervane suggests.

"My friend, we are not like Christian monks. We have families, but the key is not to get trapped in our fleeting passions. It is to remember that there is something more, something larger that holds great meaning and lasts eternally. And to hold fiercely to that desire alone. Then even our lust can be channeled toward God via true repentance. It can be a part of the way to Him."

"And the unbelievers?" Pervane asks, "those deniers of truth?"

"Non-Muslims long for God too, Pervane They may not know it yet, so they believe this world is all there is and long for comfort or relief from illness or marital love. But beneath those longings, all men yearn for God and desire to see Him face to face."

"But Master," Iqbal interjects, "I have so many questions. I desire answers -- answers that will make my heart still."

"No, Iqbal, it's not God's way to answer every question singly. By one answer all questions will be resolved."

The moon shines its silvery fullness over the domed hall of the mosque. Facing in the direction of Mecca, his son bends his knee before him. Velad is the image of his younger self: smooth, dark skin, a long nose and lanky arms and legs. His beard has grown in, his shoulders have broadened, and he is now nearly as tall as he is. Velad is ready to wear the turban.

Rumi lifts the white fabric, measures a length of it with his arm, and brings it to his lips. Feeling a smile cross his face, he pins it to the back of Velad's head and uses his other hand to wrap it toward his left ear, then toward his right. Coiling it round and round in layers until Velad's skullcap and hair are completely covered, Rumi tucks in the end piece on the bottom, steps back, and examines his son.

Velad's head wobbles for a moment from the unfamiliar weight, as he peers back at him.

"Son, today, you are a man. A man does not become scholarly simply by wearing a turban. Scholarship is a quality of essence. May you grow wise, Velad."

"I will try, God willing," he replies, kissing Rumi's hand and sitting back on the prayer rug.

"And today," Rumi adds as he lowers himself to the carpet beside his son, "you need to learn more of our family story because you are not only set apart as a Sufi, you are also set apart by blood. You see, my mother's ancestors can be traced back to the Prophet Mohammed himself, blessed be He. And my father claimed Abu Bakr, the first successor of the Prophet, as his ancestor.

"One night my father's father had a dream in which the Prophet told him to wed a princess. Well, of course, it was hard to imagine a poor scholar marrying a princess! But the king became my grandfather's patron and eventually gave his daughter to him. And my grandfather believed his dream had come true."

Nodding, Rumi concluded, "Nine months later, Bahaoddin was born."

"Your grandmother was a princess?" His son's keen eyes are flashing.

"Yes, Velad, and she wanted my father to become a king like hers. But, even as a boy, Bahaoddin wasn't interested in the power of the world. He was a Sufi, a hidden lover of God, and desired only the power of God. So, he waited. As the Koran says, God is with those who are patient.

"At last, at 22, Bahaoddin had a dream of the Prophet, who was sitting in a tent in the desert surrounded by his companions. The Prophet seated my father at his right hand and announced that, as of that day, he should be known as the Sultan of Scholars. When he woke up, he learned that many other men in the town had the same dream! They became his disciples, and his path opened before him, praise God."

As Velad leans back again, closing his eyes, Rumi knows that he is seeing the chain of Sufis, tall, calm men like a row of cypress trees, leading from Bahaoddin all the way back to the Prophet.

"You are a part of that chain," Rumi says solemnly, "a link in a great lineage."

The family moves again into an orderly rhythm of life. At night, a caravan of stars marches across the sky. At sunrise, the song of prayer tolls in the reception area.

For breakfast, they gather before a tray to eat bread and a few olives and dates with goat's milk. Rumi studies them: Velad has an inwardness about him, his attention moving naturally away from the objects of the world and toward his soul. He reads constantly yet knows instinctively that words will never satisfy him.

Aloeddin, his round face and light skin like his mother's, now has a wisp of wiry beard. He exudes nervousness and continually rubs his big right ear, as if he wants to pin it down to his head. Obedient and pious, he is more concerned with the *Shari'a* than with his inner world.

Kira, whose cheeks are now marked with soft lines, radiates the same strength she showed on the day they met. And something more, an unknown depth that is shrouded from him, making her more difficult to read than his followers or his sons.

Kimiya, his adopted daughter, has grown from girl to woman over night. No longer content to tip toe beside Kira's skirts, she appears restless and discontent, her face constantly changing like the weather.

Just then, Aloeddin smiles at Kimiya with dancing eyes. She titters, withdraws her glance, and fixes it on the brown bread and tiny black olives on the tray. Reaching out and placing an olive in her mouth, she sets her hand back in her lap and chews slowly.

"Come, sister," Aloeddin suggests, "I'll teach you to read some sweet verses from the holy book."

Together with Kira, they get up, clear the tray, and move toward the women's quarters. Vegetable vendors arrive with their donkey carts full of produce: green-stemmed leeks, bitter white turnips, rosy wrinkled pomegranates, sleek purple eggplants. Rumi can hear Kira in the kitchen beating heaps of dry chickpea plants with a stick to free them from the pods.

When someone knocks and requests permission to enter, he welcomes the guest and stands at the pedestal candle, as his father did each day, to receive her. Distraught and teary, the woman bends to kiss Rumi's hand and offers him a bit of black cloth from the *ka'aba* in Mecca.

"I did the *hajj*, Master. I pray and fast and give alms. But I don't have faith. I don't believe there is more than I can see. How can I believe in what I don't experience?"

Rumi has heard all this before -- the loss of faith, the reliance on the visible world. The believers are listening to philosophers who claim that human reason, rather than the Prophet's revelation, is the source of knowledge. Exasperated, he is about to cry out in frustration, "But. . ." when he catches himself, spins about to hide his impatience, and draws a breath. *God, give me patience with the doubters.*

He turns back to the woman, whose eager face is like that of a child awaiting a sweet. "My mother says I'm cursed with a *jinn* because I'm too lazy even to wash my husband's clothes. But I just don't know what's important anymore." She hangs her head in shame. "When will Allah return my faith?"

This woman depends on him now. He strokes the bristles of his beard, struggling to find the words to console her. A ladder appears in his mind's eye, stretching from beneath the earth into the heavens.

"Please, come into the kitchen where my wife cooks soup."

A hearty scent greets them. There is a pile of vegetable skins and a dish of goat milk on a tray. He goes over to the hearth and lifts the lid on a large bronze pot, asking, "You see the chickpeas in boiling water? We can't hear them, but they are complaining about their fate too. They don't know that they attain a higher station only by sacrifice. By being cooked and eaten, they take on human form. When chickpeas realize this, they'll say, 'Let me cook happily.'"

Confused, the woman squints, hangs her head again, and kicks at the stone floor.

"There are ladders everywhere," Rumi tries again. "Look at me: I was a mineral that became a plant and a plant that became animal and an animal that became a man. I will die as a man too, perhaps becoming an angel. Everything but God will perish. He alone is real."

The rhythmic words catch the woman's attention. "That would make an eloquent poem, Master."

Rumi frowns, "I'm a scholar! What do I have to do with poetry? Don't you hear the hidden meaning behind my words?"

Taken aback, the visitor apologizes, bows her head, and scuttles out of the room. *That woman is thirsty like me,* he thinks, going back to the reception area. *But she holds an empty cup, while mine has offered me a taste.*

Again, a knock at the door. A group of dervishes comes in, clustering around him at the pedestal candle. Their spokesman asks for assistance because they bought a garden to feed their families but don't have enough money to complete the purchase.

Calling Velad, he tells him to bring the sack of coins from recent donations.

"But, father," his son objects, "we need that money for seeds."

He shakes his head in silence. Velad retrieves the sack and turns it upside down. Silver *dirhams* and gold *dinars* clatter onto a tray. His son is about to apportion a part to the dervishes, but he sweeps the coins into his hands and offers them all in a heap to the Brothers.

"Go with God's blessings," he tells them as the silver and gold fall into a mound in the dervish's hands. "And feed your families."

Velad clucks his tongue and slaps his arms on his thighs in frustration.

"Son," Rumi faces him, "the world is a mountain, our action a cry whose echo comes back to us."

For Rumi, everything is in its place. As his father predicted, Sultan Kaykobad followed Bahaoddin to paradise. The new sultan, Jelaluddin Karatay, and Emir Pervane continue to pay a high tribute to the Mongols, who now control the surrounding territories as a protectorate. As a result, the city of Konya has remained untouched by violence since his Brotherhood arrived nearly fifteen years earlier.

Rumi has knowledge as wide as the sky in him. He strolls through the streets with eighteen-year-old Velad, both wearing patched blue frocks and a Koran in a leather case on a cord passing over their left shoulders, and he knows the satisfaction of fatherhood.

Even Aloeddin, who has suffered such grief, appears to have recovered from his mother's death and taken up studying again.

And yet that restlessness gnaws at him. Even here, in his own reception room, surrounded by soft cushions and rosy light, a nagging feeling of lack pursues him. *I am living my father's life, preaching sermons, teaching followers, and training my son. But there must be something more than this duty, this family, even this Brotherhood? Something more. . . .*

He carelessly drops the book he is reading at his side and sits back against the wall, knees up, head falling into his hands. Reading no longer captures him. His scholarly life is as empty as a robe on a wall hook.

He wrests his attention back to the room, back to the carpet-covered wall, back to the lumpy cushion beneath him. *My scholarly life is* not *as empty as a robe on a hook! These images distract me from my studies.*

Getting up, he darts through the door, heading toward the orchards in Meram to clear his mind. He climbs for a while until the hillside flattens onto a plateau, and the fragrance of autumn grasses comes toward him. Slowing his pace, his mind opens out into the scene. A thick green brocade supports his steps. Lemons, brown with age, cluster around the roots of their trees. Overripe apples have begun to rot in the dirt and return to their source. A small brook, lined with mint and fenugreek, races and ripples below. The blue frock of sky spreads like a dervish cloak around the orchard.

More images! A sadness wells up in him, a nostalgia that comes with this moment in the garden calling to him, calling him somewhere else.

Pressing his heels deeper into the soft earth, he yearns for completion. For unity, an end to separation. He yearns only for that. Nothing else holds meaning for him now.

His wife does not fill that hole. Neither do his sons, nor his disciples. Even his practices are not enough to fulfill him. He wants more *baqa*, more God consciousness. It alone will endure.

15

Lovers share a sacred decree –
to seek the Beloved.

For three days, beneath a date palm outside of Kaiseri, Shams of Tabriz prays without ceasing. His knees as calloused as a camel's from prostrations, his belly a hollow drum, his forehead resting on the parched earth, his mouth full of dust, he calls out to God, "If only You will show me the face of my one true friend, I will do anything." He inhales, then exhales, "If only You will show me his face, I will do anything."

"Will you give your head?" The voice travels from a long distance, yet it rings with familiarity, like the gentle call of a *muezzin* from a far off tower. It is so faint that it might have been missed in the slightest wind. But during his years of wandering and waiting, the dervish has learned to listen, and this voice awakens him to God's time and God's purpose.

"I will give my head."

"Then go to Konya. There you will find the one you seek."

Three weeks later, during an all-night vigil near Konya, Shams sees the skies sprinkle powder over the mountains, mud houses, and cypress trees. *White, everything white. But the whiteness holds a potential for green, a promise of spring. Each is hidden in the other, like the warm soul hidden in the cold body.*

With the first rays of the new day, he treads alongside the camel drivers bringing salt to town. Konya appears at first as a faint line of walls and towers that is almost imperceptible in the whiteness. The rows of vineyards just outside the city look like a stunted forest of twisted, dead twigs. But in the distance he catches the outline of glorious minarets ascending against the sky, and he feels a tentative hope ascending too. Stepping onto a drawbridge at a city gate, he crosses the moat.

Seeking a room for the night, he stops at the inn of the sugar merchants. The innkeeper leads him first to a spacious area with a woven sleeping mat, colorful cushions, and floral curtains.

Next the man shows him a smaller room appointed with a faded rug and two thin, threadbare cushions. Again, he evinces displeasure. Finally, the man creaks open a door onto a small bare cell with a balcony, and he nods in consent.

He folds his knees in a corner and buries his chin in his breast, anticipating the usual calm that arrives as a welcome guest when he turns away from outer distractions. So, when a hoarse sob escapes his throat, he is taken by surprise. A flood of emotion assails him.

Rising, Shams wraps his tattered black cloak around his shoulders, sets the pointed hat on his head, and perches like a hawk on the balcony above the street of the mirror sellers. Hours later, as the gold ornament rises high in the East, a cluster of men in blue robes approaches, circling around their *sheikh* on his donkey like pilgrims around the *ka'ba*. Shams hears a far-off clap of thunder like Gabriel's trumpet. As the crowd grows closer, fingers pointing emphatically and turbans nodding, he remains alert.

A Christian monk in a hooded robe and a Jew in a black cap enter the crowd and mingle with the dervishes. The *sheikh*, on the donkey, welcomes them all with a nod.

As they pass beneath the inn balcony, Shams can make out a few words. "He who awakens one person awakens all people."

Yes, it is true. Gathering his strength, he descends the stair and steps among them.

16

Open your eyes and come –
Return to the root of the root
of your own soul.

The desert dervish appears out of nowhere. Rumi is transfixed by his sudden, dream-like appearance. Emaciated as a reed and covered with road dust, the man's head and eyebrows are shaven clean. Draped in an old black cloak and wearing a strange, pointed hat, he carries himself like a Biblical prophet, like Moses himself, with that massive wooden staff, which he places upright on the ground between them.

Without warning, the dervish grabs the reins of his donkey and the animal startles, jostling him. His hawk eyes seem to search his own like prey.

The stranger lifts his staff and steps even closer, as Rumi feels a rising trepidation. His neck outstretched, the dervish shouts at him, "Who was greater, the Prophet Mohammed or . . ."

"Mohammed was the ocean itself."

"*Alhamdullilah*! Praise God!" The dervish's piercing cry splits the air.

Suddenly, Rumi slips down from the donkey, falling onto his back with a thud. He gazes up at feathery wisps of white floating freely, thinning almost to invisibility, and dissolving into blue. Just then, his body seems to float up, and the men and shops below recede into miniatures. The trees vanish. He enters a wide, open space in which the air is spinning about him, sweeping him up and turning him about like a gnat inside the wind. Arms outstretched, he lets go and becomes the whirling, forgetting where he is and who he is. Rising higher, becoming cloud, then pure air, then nothing – yet everything, a wind through all things, a whiff of wisteria.

He feels a sensation between the eyebrows, the touch of wood. His body jolts against the hard ground. A blazing heat goes up his back into his chest and bursts into a white light in his forehead.

Moments later, his neck itches against gritty pebbles and his throat scratches from thirst. His eyes open. Filmy thin puffs of cloud float above and dissolve. *Fana, I dissolved in fana like the clouds!*

Rumi lifts his head off the ground, and the stranger towers above him, bright sparks flickering through him. He recognizes the man, although he has never seen him before. He struggles to recall that burnt face, those eyes like live coals.

Insan al-kamil. The complete human being. The words light up in his mind. *My father's last secret! My spiritual yearning would lead me to a complete man. If I followed my* himma, *it would lead me home.*

Reaching out his arms like a child, he whispers to no one in particular, "The God that I have worshipped all my life appears to me today in human form."

Without his knowing it, the Brothers moved forward, forming a circle around him, their daggers drawn and glinting in the sunlight. Now, with his words, the crowd is silenced, the knives are sheathed.

He rises from the dirt. Without shaking the dust off his robes or looking around at his Brothers, he takes the stranger's hand and ambles away with him, the gentle warmth of the winter sun settling like a cloak on his shoulders.

In the seminary courtyard, a pool of water glistens with the reflection of a lofty cypress tree. Surrounded by a group of disciples with a few books in his arms, Rumi opens one and begins to teach, "In the name of God, the Compassionate, the Merciful. . ."

Just then, Sham passes through the portal, rushes into the courtyard, and grabs the books from him. "What are these?" he exclaims, holding them up in both hands.

Alarmed, Rumi retorts, "You wouldn't understand," then instantly regrets his response.

"Why don't you speak what you know?" the dervish persists, tossing the manuscripts into the pond. "Knowledge in the books remains in the books. What is it worth if you don't know the one important thing, the one true reality?"

The water turns inky blue.

Rumi wails, "The only copy of my father's <u>Divine Sciences</u>! And <u>The Book of Secrets</u>, a gift of Attar!"

An instant later, shamed by the terrible sting of attachment, he confesses that he did not know when he became so devoted to words on a page. *I teach that words are a shadow of reality -- but don't live it.*

With a sly grin, Shams reaches into the pond, retrieves the books one at a time, and holds each up for view. They are dry and intact. Again shock ripples through Rumi, but this time he remains silent, watching.

"This one?" Shams jeers. "Is this the one you love? You can read them for a thousand years, but if you cannot write your own text, you will remain in the dark."

Rumi hears the truth ringing. *The hidden meaning of my own teaching!*

But Iqbal is outraged. "How can these books be dry? What is this, sorcery?"

"You wouldn't understand," the dervish mimics.

Rumi is amused, but the Brothers are whispering among themselves in angry tones.

"Who needs witchcraft when God works well enough? This is *baqa*, God consciousness," he says, staring at Iqbal. "If knowledge does not liberate you from the lower self, then ignorance is better."

Shams turns his glare on him. "From now on, you are forbidden to read your father's words."

His fascination past, Rumi is overtaken by loss, the guidance of his father suddenly out of reach.

But the dervish continues, commanding him, "Now, bring me a glass of wine!"

Frozen, he is stopped for an instant, paralyzed by doubt. *Should he trust this man? Will he turn him into an infidel?*

The murmurs around him grow more urgent, the air more tense. Mehmet, looking outraged, turns toward him. "Master, may I offer the guest a glass of tea instead?"

The words arouse him. Shams is still staring at him resolutely, the gaze showering him with sunlight. Suddenly, he knows. *Wine cannot enter his mouth. It must turn to water at the touch of his lips.*

"Velad, go to the wine seller's shop and buy a small bottle."

Velad's mouth gapes open. Spinning on his heel, he dashes out of the courtyard.

Rumi's eyes are locked onto Shams' as they circle one another silently when Velad returns. His focus is broken as his son offers him the bottle and a glass.

He stops circling and takes the bottle in hand. Trembling, he pours and offers the wine to Shams.

Taking the glass, the dervish utters a shout – "*Mas'Allah!*" – and raises it to his lips. The Brothers gasp in horror.

But instead of drinking, Shams flips it over, spilling bloody fluid in a puddle. Then he rips his shirt, falls to the ground, and prostrates himself at Rumi's feet. "As a man of true submission, there is no one equal to you."

Rumi is elated. He bends down, lifts Shams to standing, and they embrace like lovers lost to each other and found again. That embrace, chest to chest, lasts for only an instant. But with it Rumi knows that he has stepped onto the path of love. *I will become a servant of the beloved. And Shams' face will be the face of God for me. Whatever the consequences.*

17

My face is yellow with regret –
    don't ask me why.
My tears are falling like the seeds of a pomegranate –
    don't ask me why.

Aloeddin was not with the Brothers that day when his father collided with the stranger. But when Rumi arrives home with a suspicious character in a pointed hat, Aloeddin scrutinizes him. The dervish seems too self-confident and aloof, strutting about while waving his staff. When the stranger tells Rumi that they should be alone, and his father obeys, closing the curtain to the reception room, Aloeddin panics. *My father, the Master, does not obey others. They obey him!*

Aloeddin peeks in at the two men, who circle one another hungrily, like animals sniffing each other's scent. There is his father, shoulders hunched under a scholar's robe, lower lip trembling, peering out from his bushy brows. His father, a man like any other yet as a *sheikh* larger somehow, brighter. And that stranger, his shaven head gleaming in the candlelight, his robes filthy, nostrils flaring.

Suddenly, the dervish begins to clap and shout as he spins around Rumi like a young boy playing the child's game of spinning walnuts. Except they *are* the walnuts.

In that moment, Aloeddin's image of his father shatters. He is a believer losing the faith of his childhood. And this wave of doubt brings with it a cold wave of shame. *If father continues to obey this man, he must respect him. If he respects him, he could love him, like Velad. If Velad is worthy of Rumi's love, if that strange dervish is worthy of Rumi's love, then why aren't I?*

As he asks himself that question, Rumi and Shams stop circling and move in a silent agreement toward the ladder to the rooftop terrace. Compelled to block his father, he darts forward, grabs Rumi's hand and clutches it, pulling the knuckles to his lips. His father retracts his hand quickly and climbs up toward the roof behind Shams.

He does not even see me. I am invisible to him.

Halfway up, Rumi turns back toward him. "Aloeddin, take your anger for a walk. You are lost in your *nafs*, forgetting that God is not absent from this moment or any moment. Go, walk it off!"

To Velad, he instructs, "Don't let anyone disturb us."

Slumped at the bottom of the stair, Aloeddin looks up toward the roof with wet eyes. He glances across the room toward the women's quarters, where he hears the muffled voices of Kira, Kimiya, and the servants. He shrugs and lets out a sigh of grief. *If I doubt father's judgment, I no longer belong here. If I doubt father's love. . . .*

Just then Jami, the cat, winds himself around Aloeddin's ankle. Rage stirs in him, erasing the last trace of shame. *Father even loves this cat more than me!* Aloeddin shakes his foot with such a force that it sends the ball of fur flying across the room.

18

*Go beyond your tangled thoughts
and find the splendor of Paradise.*

As the moon disappears entirely from the dark sky, Rumi closes the door on the world and opens the window on the heart with Shams. For forty days and forty nights, he knows no drowsiness, no sorrow. He is thirsty, running, arms open wide, into the sea.

As the hour of the evening prayer approaches on the third day, and a gray cloud floats overhead, Rumi sits across from Shams, who says, "We take about 22,000 breaths a day. Repeat 'Allah' 20,000 times, and it will burn away your thoughts."

Twenty thousand times! No room for any other thoughts. Suddenly an underlying fear of Shams, a terror of where the dervish will take him, roars to the surface. What if he becomes an infidel. . . loses his mind. . . loses everything. . . .

Just then Shams reaches into his cloak and pulls out a string of large wooden beads. "These *tesbih* beads will help you count."

Rumi clutches the smooth, hard balls in his fist, fingering each one with his thumb and index finger and pondering the instruction. What if. .

Seeming to read his mind, Shams adds, "If you get lost, just come back to the name. Always come back to His name."

Rumi begins, slowly at first, breathing in "Allah," out "Allah," gradually submitting to the name. The beads roll through his fingertips with a rattling sound, each one a reminder of Him. A fresh wind sweeps through the sky of his mind.

The sun, draped in gold brocade, rides its litter behind a cloud across the sky as his prayer changes form. Instead of pleading with God, saying His name over and over as a petition, the chant begins to take on a life of its own. When his mind wanders off to an idea or image, the name of God continues in the background. No longer need he say it; now the name says itself.

As days pass, this constant music soothes him until, one day, it moves into the foreground, and his thoughts move back, effortlessly becoming softer, less pressing on his mind until only the name of God remains. A constant presence.

His chest swells. He has achieved something at last.

"Your *nafs*, those plotting demons, got you!" Shams' voice startles him. "You may be unattached to the things of the world, but you are still attached to unattachment!"

He opens his eyes, as Shams continues, "Here is the challenge: without effort, you can't progress on the path. But if you take pride in your efforts, you'll remain trapped."

In the face of this paradox, something in Rumi snaps, gives up. He sinks to his knees, arches his back, and places his forehead on the cold, hard rooftop. The stars wheel above. A great peace descends, caressing him.

The harsh season has stolen the petals from the flowers and the fruits from the trees. Tall snowdrifts are piling up on the streets, blanketing the city below in silence.

Rumi's knees ache from sitting still for so long in the cold, but he pays no heed to the discomfort. Peering ardently into the engraved face of his beloved, he wonders where this love will lead him. This love that he clings to so fiercely, this love that has overturned his life.

He vowed never to adore anyone again, never to grasp onto a human being with attachment. Each time he suffered, he learned. And yet *this* love for Shams is more than human somehow, more than a mortal desire.

I have no choice but to submit. My heart has become my instrument, this love, my path. Wherever it goes, I will follow.

When it is no longer night but not yet day, Rumi is still crying out, exhausted, "Allah! Allah."

A freezing gale howls through the city. The sun rises, melting the ice in the streets, turning it to puddles and disappearing again, splashing yellow overhead. The tea left outside the door to the rooftop terrace grows cold. Rumi's cat, Jami, whines and scratches until he cracks open the door. She slips in and curls up at his side.

After sitting knee to knee for timeless days, breathing one breath with his friend, Shams stands above him, takes his hand, and pulls him to his feet. Arms outstretched, head gazing up at the stars, Shams begins to turn. And turn and turn.

Surprised, he starts to object to the dance. But before he can utter a word, Shams silences him – *shush!* The only sound, the dervish stamping his feet.

At Shams' urging Rumi joins him, stamping and turning, stamping and turning on the rooftop beneath the sky's black tent. He lingers in each moment, giving it his full presence. His mind, his breath, his heartbeat slow down. He enters a state of prayer, offering everything to Him. As his body turns, it joins the glistening stars in their turning and the tiny atoms in their turning. Revolving, Rumi stamps his feet and feels himself lift off the ground. The scholar turns. . . and becomes the dancer. The beloved turns. . .and becomes the lover. With each revolution, layers of his old self fall away.

With a final stamp, Shams stops. Silence, a mighty sound. They stand face to face, heated, eyes sparkling.

Shams says, "The steps of the *sema* are like the steps of pressing grapes. The dance produces a spiritual wine, the sweetness of divine life."

"My Shams, my God, you are the way."

19

Don't try to find love
*   by leaning on the cane of the intellect;*
That cane is nothing
*   but a blind man's stick.*

The moon grows fat and round. At the mosque, Rumi's students wait with growing impatience for him, roaming about day after day on the carpeted floor and grumbling to each other.

"The Master has deserted us," groans one, as he throws up his arms in exasperation.

"He has abandoned his duties and betrayed his loyalties," sneers another.

"He has fallen into spiritual delusion," snorts an old man, shaking his head.

The Brothers have lived for so long with Rumi at the hub of their lives that, without him, the circle begins to fall apart. They have lived for so long with his sermons as their spiritual nourishment, his guidance as their compass, that without him they feel starved and lost.

That night, three weeks into Rumi's retreat, Iqbal, a carpet maker, leaves his Brothers at the mosque just after dusk and trudges his way home on the slushy road. His rail-thin legs quiver, and his breath forms clouds before him. But the icy air means that snow will bring water, and that brings relief to Iqbal even after all these years. When he lived in Isfahan, snow thaws meant there was less chance of drought, so there was less chance of hunger for a boy who never had his fill of rice.

Iqbal ruminates as he makes his way in the growing darkness, trying not to step on crumbling dung patties that were not washed away in the storm. Perhaps he should have remained a sober Shi'ite like his father, strictly following the law. Perhaps he lost his way as a Sufi, trying to follow the heart.

Ever since his father taught him how to weave *kilims*, how to pluck threads through the loom, insert the comb, pull down on the pile, and tie knots that will hold for years to come, he felt gratitude for his trade. Leaving patterns of roses and blossoms to the women weavers, he became an expert in eyes, to protect against evil, and in birds, images of the soul.

But earlier that morning, as he sits at the loom to weave a prayer niche into the center of a carpet, his hands will not obey him. The knots will not hold. He tries to soothe himself by recalling his mother's faraway garden, those white-flowering vines clinging to the fountain, that resonating sound of doves cooing. But the memory, which usually calms him, brings no relief. His mind frets.

In every carpet we weave a knot of white – a tiny mistake -- into the perfect pattern of color. Shams is the mistake in the tapestry of Konya!

As Iqbal approaches Rumi's house, red-hot resentment burns in him, and he growls under his breath, "I curse that old man, Shams of Tabriz." Picking up clods of dirt, he pitches them at the house. "May he be damned for stealing our Master."

20

Even the water of life
is jealous of the tears
that fall from the lover's eyes.

Meanwhile, inside the house, Rumi's wife continues to wait for her husband. Kira should have been pounding wheat or churning butter. She should have been helping Sepahsalar in the vegetable garden or Kira with the washing. Instead, she sits near the door as dusk falls, listening for his footsteps. Only the twittering and calling of the night creatures greet her.

She goes to the kitchen and ladles some lentils and rice into a bowl, preparing his dinner to bring him home. Heating his favorite tea, she adds a bit of clove and sets the meal on a tray in the reception area. Then she crosses her legs on a cushion and waits, as the food grows cold.

Kira needs the balm of Rumi's presence. Without him she has no purpose, no direction for her prayers. Without him she is no one.

As she has done many times now, she leaves the tray abandoned and lies down to rest early. Although her muscles ache with tiredness, her mind is alert, groping for answers. Gradually, she slips into the empty gap between waking and sleeping.

She is stretched out beside him again, her small head in the nook of his shoulder. She raises her head and moves her open mouth down from his mouth, touches her lips on his hard chest, then on his fuzzy belly. She moves her mouth down toward it, an open mouth, waiting, longing to be filled. Her mouth, an empty vessel, waiting to be filled, a baby bird, open mouth, ready, open.

"Open wide," he says. It's the perfect width for her, the perfect head, wild mushroom, setting high on long stalk, mouth open, ready, waiting. Waiting to be filled, tiny bird, open mouth, take it in, open wider, filling her with the waters of life.

Flushed, Kira awakens with an urgent need to see her husband. She climbs up to the rooftop terrace and stands outside the door, believing that he will need to use the latrine eventually. Time passes, her legs ache, then he appears and tries to dart past her.

She touches his arm, whispering, "Dear one, you are needed here. Your sons await you. Your disciples await you. I await you in our bed." She pulls the pin from her hair and lets it fall around her face.

He pulls back, looking offended, then forcing his glance past her. She knows she has lost.

"Kira, be as patient as Zuleikha. She longed for Joseph like the soul longs for God. The idea of him kept her alive until she was united with him."

At fifteen, when Kira, the eldest of nine daughters, is summoned to her father's room at their home in Ephesus, she feels dread, suspecting that a wealthy Muslim who has been watching her had contacted her father. She shudders as she is told that the man offered her family a good price for her on one condition: to become his third wife, she must convert to Islam.

"But, father, I don't want to marry him or move away from you. Not yet, please."

"Daughter, this is not about you. You must consider the whole family."

An exchange has already been made. *And what did you receive for the price of my life?*

"Conversion will not be difficult, Kira." Her father's words break into her shock. "The Muslims believe in prayer, fasting, and tithing, just as we do. They even go on pilgrimage to the holy land – but to Mecca, not Jerusalem. And they believe that Mohammed came after Jesus as a prophet. Who knows?" he shrugs. "Maybe he did."

Her head dizzy, Kira hears herself whispering, "Yes, father" but does not know who mouths the words.

A few minutes later, she hurries down the smooth marble road that the Romans built for their chariots. When she was younger, she loved to slip and slide over its smoothness on her way to church, imagining that the men who built it paved the way just for her. The salty scent of the sea from Pamucak beach fills the air, telling her that she is getting closer to her destination.

As she leaves the road and scrambles up the slopes toward the basilica of St. John, she recalls the story she heard in childhood. At his crucifixion, Jesus asked his disciple, John, to look after his mother. John and the Virgin came to Ephesus and, after his death, a small church was dedicated to him there. But in the sixth century the emperor built a much larger church over the sacred grave of St. John, and now fine dust from the grave can cure illness in believers.

At the entrance to the basilica on the west wall, Kira holds her breath. She will never see this beautiful place again. Shaped in the form of a cross, it has four domes supported on columns running the length of it and a pair flanking the central dome above the saint's tomb. There is a semicircular row of seats where the priests sit during ritual. The colors in the mosaic floors and the wall paintings north of the tomb have not faded. To her, the church is grander than the buildings of the Greeks and Romans who came centuries before, grander even than the Muslim mosque with its courtyard and pool just down the hill. Kneeling before the great cross, Kira holds her face in her hands and weeps.

Eight years later, she is a widow in Konya. Now, though her husband is alive, she feels like a widow again.

21

I am a lover of love.
I am a mighty lion
thinking I am a lamb.

After forty days, Aloeddin observes Rumi and Shams step down the ladder into the reception area. Crowds of people await his father and speak all at once, each pleading a cause: family duties, teaching duties, petitions to the sultan.

Moving to the pedestal candle, Rumi holds up a hand, and they are silenced. *At least they still obey him.*

"My sons and daughters, before the arrival of Shams, I was raw. Then I got cooked. Now I want burning!"

The Brothers look at each other quizzically. His father reaches over to the wall niche and picks up a book, raising it high, then letting it drop to the floor with a thump. "Enough of books! Enough of philosophy! This is the time for love!"

Startled, Aloeddin stifles himself. Several Brothers scowl. Another paces about, hands on his hips. Anxious anticipation fills the air.

Mehmet steps forward, "Yes, Master, but when will the discourses begin again?"

Shams roars, "Rationality -- nothing comes of it! It may take you to the door of truth, but when you want to enter the house, it's nothing but a veil."

His father's discourses a veil? Aloeddin cannot believe what he hears.

Shams casts a harsh look at the Brothers. "Do you know what love is?" he challenges them. "If you're like us, you'll know it! If not, you're lost!"

Just then, Rumi steps forward and, with one swift motion, lifts off the dark gown that signifies his scholar's rank by its wide sleeves. Handing the robe to him, his father declares, "Aloeddin, put this away forever, and bring the tailor here. I need a new robe, a green one. I am new."

He is paralyzed, the robe hanging on his arm, a dead weight.

His father begins to dance through the crowd, springing lightly on his feet, much like a deer. As he greets each person, he bows.

He submits to them now? He submits to mere human beings? The rage in him boils, but his inner ranting is interrupted by his father's words.

"From now on, all of you will obey Shams, my *sheikh*."

Aloeddin watches, indignant, as Velad steps out from the crowd, approaches Shams, bends his knee, and kisses the dervish's right hand. Salaoddin, a goldsmith, also moves forward and bows deeply, followed by Husamoddin, a tall, young novice, and Sepasahlar, the servant.

Two others nod to one another, turn their backs, and stride out the door, letting it slam shut.

I must speak up. I must try one last time to reach him. "Father, Shams does not wear the patched robe of the Order."

"Son, his cloak comes from the Prophet himself. Shams is a hidden saint."

"But, father, he is impatient and intolerant. He is criticizing the learned men of Konya."

"And you are criticizing him. Aloeddin, if you see a fault in another, it is within yourself. Get rid of that fault in you, and you will see him differently. Remember, each of us is a mirror of the other."

Appearing to dismiss his concerns, his father turns toward the room. "Understand what I tell you. I have known Shams before. He is the guide of light, the saint of Sufis. I dreamed of him, not this fierce one who wandered for forty years to find me but the mythical beloved whose heart is polished to clear reflection. Secretly, I longed for him, hunting him as he hunted me. Then he stood in front of me – as Shams of Tabriz."

Aloeddin falls to his father's feet, defeated.

Without seeming to notice him, Rumi concludes, "Everything before that moment faded into the past. I stepped into the present, the eternal present. What can I do – but bow and submit?"

Silence.

The tension leaks out of the room. Several men fall to sitting, a woman weeps. And a sigh of acceptance rolls through the air.

His father begins again, his voice gentler now. "We will build a special hall to do *sema*, the sacred turning."

A few listeners grumble their objections, but the anger is gone now, and Rumi proceeds. "The roof of the hall will be open to the stars. The musicians can have their own gallery, and the sound of their music will fill the *medrasa*."

Aloeddin simply shakes his head in silence.

"After all," Rumi continues, "music is the creaking of the doors of paradise."

"But Master," a Brother tries, "I don't like the sound of creaking doors."

"I hear the doors as they open," Rumi smiles. "You hear them as they close."

His message complete, his father begins moving through the crowd, greeting people, and bowing to each one. Arriving in front of Fakhrun Nisa, he bows low, as Aloeddin feels resentment rising like a fire in his chest. *The first woman disciple.*

" *Asalaam alaykum*, my daughter," Rumi says.

"And peace on you, Master," she replies.

"Is there something you wish to ask?" He pauses, looking at her intently. "Oh, you wish to make the pilgrimage to Mecca. God willing, we will be there together."

Fakhrun appears stunned but says nothing.

Rumi dismisses the others and invites her to remain as a guest. Several hours later, in the reception room below, Aloeddin is awakened by his father's shouts for her to come up to the rooftop. "Fakhrun Nisa, come, come and see your wish come true."

Fakhrun, roused from sleep and wrapped in a robe, climbs the stair. Aloeddin hears a screech, then a thud.

A moment later, looking shaken and pale, Fakhrun steps down and enters the reception room, still unsteady on her feet. Just then,

Velad rushes in and offers her a cushion. Alert, Aloeddin stands aside.

"It was the *ka'aba*," she says breathlessly to his brother. "First, he knew I wanted to make the pilgrimage. Then he took me there, to the black stone. It was spinning in the sky above!"

Velad's jaw drops. Then he leans forward, "What did my father say?"

Aloeddin moves closer. "He told me," she gulps, "when you follow the path of the law, you must go to Mecca and circle the *ka'aba*. But when you follow the path of love, here is where you find the beloved."

"Where?" Velad demands.

"Here," Fakhrun taps her own heart, saying under her breath. "He said, the inner pilgrim circles the *ka'aba* of the heart. That is the hidden meaning of the *hajj*."

Aloeddin does not know what happens to his father in those endless retreats with Shams. But in that moment he is certain of their results. *Rumi has succumbed to spiritual pride. He stopped a disciple from making the holy pilgrimage that is required by the Prophet himself. My father is doomed.*

22

I saw and I touched –
My whole face became eyes,
    all my eyes became hands.

A week later, Shahid is invited to Rumi's house for the evening meal. He anticipates a secret universe opening up to him, a world of piety, self-control, and honor. A world of Brotherhood. Elated but apprehensive, he stands at the master's door and notices the aloe hanging as a talisman to ward off evil spirits. *Perhaps it's an omen that the dirty dervish will not be here.*

After receiving permission to enter, Shahid joins a few men squatting on the floor of the reception room around a large silver tray. Shams is among them, his shaven skull shining, his odd hat resting beside him, his long staff within reach. *That walking stick is dangerous. It might drive people away or, perhaps, like Moses's wand, turn into a serpent.*

Dressed in a new green robe, Rumi leans into Shams, two trees in a breeze. Velad, relaxed at his father's other side, wears muslin pants and a white vest that is inscribed with verses from the Koran. He looks just like a younger version of his father. Mehmet is there too, his dark face wet with perspiration, his rotund body resting like a stuffed cushion on the floor. And the novice, Husamoddin, whose long, thin legs, draped in a blue cloak, look like a bowl beneath him. Aloeddin, in patched robes, sits away from the others, his round eyes staring off into space, his round mouth pouting, a large ear sticking out from his turban. Only he seems restless, his fingers tapping the carpet.

The Brothers place narrow towels on their laps. Their right knees raised, their left flat on the floor, and their right arms bare to the elbow, they tuck up the ends of their sleeves. Passing around a copper bowl full of water, they wash their right hands, and Shahid follows suit.

"*Bismillah*, in the name of God," Rumi begins. Aloeddin pushes himself closer to the tray as the other men pick up rice between their thumbs and fingers, press it into a wad, and place it into their mouths. The pilaf tastes sweet and chewy to Shahid. There is stew with spinach and cheese with flat bread too.

Rumi turns to Shams, "Would you like to speak to the Brothers, my *sheikh?*"

The dervish responds, "Let's discuss the real meaning of *sheikh*. A disciple is a real disciple only when he loses himself in the *sheikh* and attains *fana*. But, for that to happen, the *sheikh* has to be free on the inside. On the outside, he goes to the market, but inside he is in union with God."

Rumi adds, "Some novices are beguiled by impostors, believing them to be united with God. But they don't know the difference between fact and fiction."

"Yes," Shams sneers. "They praise a person who isn't even worthy of carrying their shoes!"

Shahid notices that Velad has not eaten much. He seems to smell the fragrance of truth in the words. Aloeddin, on the other hand, eats hungrily and hardly hears the words. He is transported by the coolness of cucumber on his tongue.

Just then, Rumi interrupts Aloeddin's feast. "Son, you enjoy the food so much, yet you are never filled. Put down your spoon and go get more water for our guest to drink."

Grumbling, Aloeddin rubs his ear, shoots a look at his father, and gets up, carrying the pitcher to the kitchen.

Mehmet puts down a spoon and says, "Master, some of our friends are losing patience with the Sufi path." He hesitates. "They're saying that the darkness will never turn to dawn, so they are using hashish. And now they believe they are having angelic visions without the guidance of a *sheikh*."

A growl sounds from Shams' throat. "Don't get near those who are led by their desires. Those visions are of no value -- they are born from the Evil One himself."

"But," Mehmet tries to object, "wine is forbidden in the Koran and hashish is not."

"There was a cause for every verse of the holy book," Shams explains. "Hashish was not consumed during the time of the Prophet, blessed be He. That's why He didn't need to forbid it. Brother, you must not obey your bodily desires. They must obey you."

Silence falls like a curtain over the room. Shahid struggles to envision his desires, his tyrannical *nafs*, obeying him.

Mehmet edges away from the tray, washes his hands and mouth to complete the meal, and holds out the bowl to Aloeddin for him to wash. Husamoddin receives it from him.

But Shahid, his lips wet with watermelon juice, does not want to stop eating.

"It's nearly time for evening *zikhr*, little Brother," Rumi says to him.

Reluctantly, he washes up too.

Kira enters the room and serves hot tea. The men kiss the glasses before they sip, causing him to raise his brows in surprise.

"Shahid," Rumi explains, "we greet the glass with a kiss because it's worthy of our respect. In this way, we learn to honor Him even in material forms. Oh, this is my daughter, Kimiya," he adds, as a girl comes out from behind the curtain, quickly covering her mouth with a headscarf.

Shahid feels his cheeks flush and his stare pin on her, on her silken skin and the outline of her rounded shape, which is barely detectable beneath the folds of her robe as she bends and rises, bends and rises to clear away the meal. He fixes on her hands – small and thin and delicate – as they hold the tray. The longer he watches, the more his body awakens with tingles of forbidden sensations.

Although Kimiya keeps her glance down and does not acknowledge him in any visible way, Shahid does not feel discouraged. Drawn to her modesty, he even wonders if her avoidance of him is an indication of her interest, a secret attraction that she would not dare to betray in public.

He recalls the lost homing pigeon that he watched the day before circling frantically above Konya alone, without direction or purpose.

When the pigeon man saw the bird from his rooftop, he released several flocks, which moved like dark wrinkles across the sky. The lost one tried joining first one flock, then another until, at last, she flew toward her object -- home. *In the same way, my circling has a direction now and a purpose: Kimiya.*

23

*How could anyone touched by your love
not dance like a weeping willow?*

At seventeen, Kimiya wears a dreamy, far-off look in her eyes. The next morning, tired of helping with the women's work, she sneaks into the reception room and peeks out through a fissure in the front wall at the street below. She longs to hear the guttural sounds of foreigners, as they break words apart in strange places. She imagines strolling through the noisy *souk* with the warm sun on her back, while vendors call her to select fine fruits and pungent herbs. She envies the boys, who can go out and wander freely through the city streets. Comparison and envy are forbidden by the Koran and come from evil itself, but she cannot stop her longings now.

Peering through the crack, her hands flat against the wall beside her head, Kimiya envisions the most dangerous scene: she is promenading down the street, flowers cradled in her arms, when a handsome boy catches her attention. And she looks back. Both of them know in that moment that they understand each other.

Three years earlier, on the new moon, Kimiya awakens to find red fluids flowing down her thigh in a sticky stream. Certain she is dying, she runs to her mother, who gives her a rag and tells her that she is now a woman who can bear children.

In the other hand, her mother offers her a blue headscarf, like her own. "This *hijab* will keep any man but your husband from seeing your hair. Sufis don't require women to wear the veil because there is no law in the Koran that our faces and hands must be covered. But we wear the scarf for modesty."

When Kimiya learns that the blood means she is impure and cannot handle the Koran at those times, she chokes back sobs and goes to find Rumi in the reception room.

"Please, father, may I pray even though the blood is here?"

"Kimiya, according to the law, you may not touch the sacred book during times of impurity. You are freed from fasting and formal prayer to make it easier at those times, but you may continue to pray if you wish."

Now a woman for a full three years, her fantasies are growing bolder. That night on her sleeping mat, Kimiya feels the swelling of her breasts and the gnawing in her belly. Lifting her hands, she lets them wander over the tiny buds blooming on her chest. Her palms rest on the bristle between her legs, which curls in tight circles. She dreams that her rug catches fire and surrounds her with a burning wall of heat.

When dawn touches the seam between this world and heaven, Kimiya awakens. A puddle of perspiration has formed in the curve of her lower back.

Following her prayers, she goes to the well behind the house with a pitcher held high. A few strands of honey-colored hair dangle from beneath her *hijab*. Letting the sleeve of her gown slip down past her elbow, her nakedness is revealed in an instant. A hot flash of shame rises up her neck to her face.

As she covers her arm and hurries to draw up the water, she scolds herself. *I must be an evil girl, an ungrateful daughter.* "Allah, forgive me, I beg you," she pleads aloud. "I vow to obey whatever duty requires of me."

She puts on her obedient smile, which men can read any way they wish. That smile is as effective as a veil. And she lets her body sink beneath the robes, shoulders slouched, chest sunk, hips forward, until she disappears in the folds as she moves toward the house.

Her bold fantasy is long gone now, stashed away in the cellar of forgotten dreams. Instead, she will follow the law Shari'a and obey her male guardians. And when she marries, she will obey her husband.

Yet, secretly, it gnaws at her that a man can leave his wife without reasons, whereas a wife can divorce her husband only if he is impotent, mad, or fails to support her financially. *And besides, a man can marry four wives and have slave concubines!*

She shakes her head violently to try to clear it. "Whoever my husband will be, please make him a kind man, God willing, to the end of his days."

24

When you move around the Soul of souls,
you become that eternal treasure.

A moonless sky greets the Brothers as they complete their ablutions in silence. Shahid does not look forward to Shams leading *zikhr* and teaching *sema* for the first time tonight. He wants the Master to remain *sheikh*. After all, he took his vow of allegiance to Rumi. And to Rumi alone.

In his black cloak and pointed hat, Shams stands at the door of the new dance hall in a strange posture and insists that each Brother imitate him as he enters. "This is the posture of humility," he says to Shahid, directing him to cross his right arm over his left, with both hands resting on his shoulders, and to bow his head toward his chest. Then Shams indicates for him to regard his feet: Shams' big right toe is placed over his left. They bow to one another, and Shahid crosses the threshold.

The others file in that way and line the edges of the hall, crossing their arms and feet. The hand-scrubbed wooden floor reflects a glint of starlight through the window. Red, blue, and green carpets cover the mats that serve as seats around the edges of the room. Their colors seem to Shahid to be unusually bright in the glare of the oil lamps. A few Brothers stare up through the open roof to the blazing stars. Others scan the walls, where scripted verses of the Koran hang.

Rumi enters and bows to each man, who bows in return. But, to Shahid's surprise, the Master does not move to the *sheikh*'s sheepskin post, which belonged to his father, but joins the others, waiting.

Shams bows at the threshold, strides to the seat of honor, folds his legs beneath him, places his pointed hat and wooden staff at his side, and ignores the suspicious stares. He and Rumi bend forward to kiss the floor, which each brother repeats as he takes a seat, forming a circle with the others, knee to knee.

Shahid feels so disturbed by these alterations in the routine for *zikhr* that he studies Rumi's face to calm himself. Tiny lines crease his forehead, gray shadows cross his cheeks, and small specks of white appear in his beard. His green robe drapes down his arms and folds across his knees. In the Master's serene presence, his nervous fears subside. *Perhaps it is the certainty of Rumi's beliefs that is so comforting to me. Or perhaps it is his kindness that allows me to relax deep inside.*

Rumi quietly explains the intention of *zikhr* practice, meditating on the ninety-nine names of God. "The divine name carries a divine presence, which takes root in us when the name takes root in our minds. One day, union with His name becomes union with Him. Now you, my *sheikh*," he concludes, nodding to Shams to continue the teaching. And with that he stands up and goes out the door.

Mehmet's eyes follow him longingly, Shahid observes. But Shams' voice calls them both to attention. "When the breath goes out through the left nostril, on *'La illaha,'* let go of your grasping, your feelings of unease. When the breath goes in through the right nostril, on *'illa'llah,'* the presence of God enters with it."

Irritated, Shahid squirms. *I never agreed to receive teachings from Shams. Now he is my sheikh's sheikh! And I have no choice but to obey.*

In his black cloak, his head bare, Shams begins the *zikhr*, "*la illhaha illa'llah.*"

Shahid breathes out – *La illaha* -- and in – *'illa*. . .and Kimiya's face rises up. His chest tightens. He exhales and reaches out to her silky cheek.

Her image seems to fit so easily into a part of him that has known only night – and now knows dawn. Pining, he recalls a childhood tale about Majnun, whose all-consuming longing for Layla sent him wandering in the desert of madness, calling out her name, "Layla, Layla," with every breath.

I am like that Majnun. My longing is not for divine love; it is for human love. My need is not to transcend; it is to belong.

Suddenly, Shams' gruff voice assaults him. "Shahid, abandon your desires. You don't have your concentration on God. Begin again

114

and remain seated until you have completed one hundred repetitions with full presence."

Ashamed, he folds into himself and begins mechanically to repeat the divine name, but it feels dry on his tongue. He longs for honey water and wonders what will be served for the evening meal.

To the others he hears Shams say, "Breathe. Say the name. Breathe. Say the name. . . .The breath between the breaths is where it all happens. The mind chatter stops, the body buzzing stops, stillness prevails. All paths lead to Mecca, the divine reality."

At the sound of footsteps, Shahid lifts his lids just slightly. The local *muezzin*, Hamza, who recently learned to play the reed-flute, is taking his place against the wall. Slowly, other musicians join him.

Rumi re-enters the hall wearing a long dark skirt, which is edged along the hem with a wool band that weighs down the bottom. It is bound at the waist with a white cumberbund, which holds down a panel of his black jacket. And he wears a tall, cone-shaped, honey-colored felt hat.

Husamoddin is staring at the Master with a slight grin, appearing to adore him. Iqbal, his forehead glistening beneath his white turban, his bony fingers flittering about, glances nervously at Mehmet. The rotund Arab nods back.

The reed-flute sings a nightingale's longing in the spring air. "Come into the *sema*," Shams' voice rings out above the music. "The lovers of God who dance here pass beyond this world to a higher truth."

Shahid draws in a breath, pretending to finish his *zikhr*. A few Brothers lean forward, transfixed by the lesson. Others pull back into themselves, apparently afraid to participate in a forbidden rite.

Shams goes on, "Focus on your left foot, revolving in a full circle with each step. Inwardly pronounce the name of God, while feeling your connection through the *sheikh* to the whole lineage. And turn with a deep love of God in your heart."

Pausing, Shams lifts his hands from his thighs and turns them upward. "You can see it's impossible to accomplish this through your will alone. You must let Him take over, so the *sema* becomes a lesson in surrender."

"But Master, some *sheikhs* say this dance is forbidden." The young novice sounds timid but sincere to Shahid's ear.

"Son, lovers of God have held spiritual concerts for two hundred years. It's not dance that induces ecstasy, but ecstasy that arouses the dance. The body that moves for pleasure will surely burn in hell. But the hands of Sufis that rise in *sema* will reach paradise, for we are danced by God the Exalted. Rise. Join me."

The Brothers form a circle, while Rumi praises the Prophet, messenger of Allah, and invokes Bahaoddin, Sultan of Scholars, and Shamsoddin, the Sun. At the first strike of the kettledrum, Shams and Rumi stoop down, slap the floor with their hands, and rise up to symbolize the day of judgment and the resurrection. Shahid and the others join in.

Shoulder to shoulder, the Brothers circle the room counterclockwise. Each time a man arrives at the sheepskin post where Shams stands, he gazes between the dervish's eyebrows.

A young boy, perhaps ten years of age, arrives before Shams at the post. He stands only as high as the dervish's waist.

"No!" Shams dismisses the boy from the dance. "Not old enough."

A few moments later, in rotation, Iqbal stands before Shams and prepares for the internal greeting.

"No!" the dervish cries. All heads turned toward Shams. "Not spiritually prepared."

Iqbal blanches and recoils, backing off the dance floor into a corner of the room.

When Rumi reaches the post, he bows to Shams in the posture of humility, then kisses his beloved's hand. Lifting off his black cloak, he drops it to the floor and arises in white. Stepping backward from Shams, he begins to turn on his left foot, whirling about as the Brothers watch.

With his index finger drawing a circle in the air, Shams indicates to each Brother, one by one, to begin the turn. As the music rises in pitch, the men open their arms, right hand up, left down. They turn round and round like bees in a house full of honey.

Shahid sits alone, as always, his mind taunting him with doubts. *What is this dervish doing to Rumi? What is the point of this dance?*

When Shams indicates that it is his turn, Shahid gets up and mimics the others. Trying to balance on the left foot, use the right to gain speed and his arms to maintain equilibrium, he spins around for a moment, and Kimiya's face floats by. Dizziness sweeps him away. He no longer knows what he is circling. Stepping backward, he collapses against the wall, breathless and embarrassed.

Rumi turns with a gentle step, lifting up into the clouds. He feels light enter through his right palm, pass through his body, and move out his left palm into the earth. His mind dissolves as his body floats up, the sounds of the dulcimer, rubaab, and reed-flute swirling around him, supporting his flight. *Fana*!

He turns again -- and becomes all that he was not. The threads of his life pull. The story unravels. And the one he disdained -- the intoxicated lover, the ecstatic dancer -- is born in him, a mirror image.

Rumi submits, letting the music turn him. He does not move of his own volition. Rather, it plays him like a viol until nothing separate remains in him.

The turning stops, and the recitation of the first chapter of the Koran begins. He prays in front of Shams, "May the grace of God and the spiritual aspiration of men be witnessed in us. For the sake of the blessed breath of our Master, Shams of Tabriz, let us say, '*Нииии.*'"

25

God is great and compassionate,
but if you plant barley,
        don't expect a harvest of wheat.

Earlier, Aloeddin reluctantly followed the others to the dance hall. He scorns the practice of music and dancing, but it has eaten its way into the Order, threatening to become a fatal disease. As he watches, scowling, the moan of the reed-flute sounds like the cry of a desperate child.

His anger rising, he turns – and strides toward the mosque. Entering the empty, vaulted hall stealthily, he winds his way around the arched columns until he reaches his father's pulpit. Then, holding his breath, he lifts a foot and carries himself up to the top.

Looking out, Aloeddin imagines the mosque filled with believers, *sheikhs*, and Koran reciters in black robes, their turbans bending toward him. Spreading his arms wide to spread the fear of God, he warns them, "This dancing is dangerous. If it arouses your passions even for a moment, your *nafs* will take control. Then how will you enter paradise? You will be punished like an unbeliever."

Nodding and murmuring their assent, his invisible followers revere him for his return to the old ways before *sema*, when right was right and wrong was wrong. He alone persuades the believers to turn, turn away from the mystical path, *Tariqa*, and turn again toward the law, *Shari'a*.

Father will not be my Master anymore. The realization rings in him. *I will submit only to the Prophet and his revelation. I will cite only the Holy Book and avoid innovation at all cost. As the Prophet said, every novelty is innovation, and every innovation is error.*

That alone is the true Islam, the true submission. That alone will be his faith. And for his holy acts he will be praised and lauded.

As the hollowness in his chest vanishes, he steps down and wanders out into the mist. Striding back toward the dance hall, he dreams of marching on and on until he reaches Mecca, enters the holy city arm in arm with thousands of pilgrims, circles the perfect black *ka'aba* as the stars circle the heavens, and offers prayers in his mother's name. He recalls hearing from a *sheikh* that a good act at Mecca is rewarded one hundred thousand times in the next world, ensuring that he will go to paradise.

Aloeddin knows then that he wants the rewards of religion, not the hidden meanings. His soul is Muslim, not Sufi.

26

The face of your religion
covers the face of His love.

Doing his ablutions, Omar carefully avoids splashing his eyes with water. He remembers when, as a youth in Basra, he wanted to be a bird seller like his father, strolling through the *souk* with gray, green-necked pigeons on his shoulders, encircled by sweet chirping sounds. But when his mother died of the pox, his father disappeared into silence, letting the birds fall over, one by one, into silence too.

When Omar was eight, the old man brought him to a nearby *medrasa* and left him there as punishment for his evil *nafs*. Did his father know that he was the only Sunni there?

The Shi'a boys chased him and taunted him until, one bright afternoon, with the sun overhead, a big, muscular bully pinned him down and, towering over him, dared him to try to run. Omar kicked up into the boy's belly and galloped off like a horse. But, at the last second, another boy stuck out his leg and tripped him. Omar fell on his face, a wooden stake piercing his left eye so that his eyeball hung beneath the socket.

But he did not cry out or whine like a baby. He cupped his hand over his eye and marched off, not looking back, although the pain was excruciating. *And even today I do not wince when recalling it.*

Even with only one eye, Omar memorized the Koran and became a Koran reciter as good as any other. He learned about Shi'a Islam and its *imams*, finding the one true faith, whose lineage goes all the way back to Ali. It is also the teaching that their enemies wish to destroy – those Christians, who believe in the Prophet Isa but refuse to accept the final Prophet and His revelation. Those Mongols, who burn the pages of His book. Even those Sunnis, who believe that their *imams* are mere prayer leaders, not the true descendants of Mohammed.

But mockers will be mocked and persecutors will be pained, as He said. All in good time.

Finished with his ablutions, Omar dabs his hollow eye socket with a cloth and sets off for the *medrasa*. Last night the Turkish sultan's guards rounded up three of his Shiite brothers and put them in prison. They were attacking the authority of the ruler, who lives in luxury while claiming to be a believer.

That Kaykobad is a hypocrite, doing prayers while making bargains with the unbelievers, who do not distinguish between clean and unclean. Those Mongols even claim that their mullah *travels to the other world and speaks to them with the voices of the dead!*

It's our duty, as true Muslims, to revolt against Kaykobad and other rulers who fail to create a proper Islamic state. We must find sheikhs who are rightful heirs of the Prophet, blessed be he, and end this corruption.

Now he is eager to hear what his *imam* has to say. *Imam* al-Farabi, an authority on the Koran and a reflection of God's attributes, did not issue a *fatwa* to rebuke the sultan. But with three members of his mosque in prison, he is sure to be raging.

Arriving at the *medrasa*, Omar passes through an open courtyard into a small dusky hall, where men in brown robes are seated on green carpets. The walls are painted with verses of the Koran, and a globe-shaped ceramic lamp hangs from the roof.

Imam al-Farabi waddles in, his robes making a swishing noise, and climbs up to the pulpit, squeezing his round, flat nose and inhaling to clear his sinus. He stares off into the distance for a moment, then focuses on Omar with a disapproving stare.

I did my ablutions and prayers tonight. Why is looking at me that way? It's a familiar feeling to him to search for a flaw inside himself.

He feels the *imam* lift his steely gaze and sighs in relief as it fall on another man. Al-Farabi proclaims, "There is no God but God. Mohammed is His messenger. 'Ali is the friend of God."

Pounding his fist on the pulpit, he bellows, "Do you know the perils of following the party of Ali, only true successor of Mohammed?" His squinting eyes search the room, and Omar casts down his glance to avoid contact.

"Do you know the bloody history of our people? How many *imams* after 'Ali were murdered in cold blood? Murdered! His son Husayn was martyred at Karbala, and every year we celebrate his martyrdom by making a pilgrimage to his tomb, God willing. The Sunnis, like the sultan, say this is idolatry. I say it is true religion!"

Omar's turban is nodding in rhythm with the others. Al-Farabi's pace is quickening. "So after the tenth successor, surrounded by killers, our *imams* became less and less available to the people. Until the twelfth *imam* – do you know his secret? At five years old, he disappeared altogether. Not just hiding from those murderers, no. Not dying as a child, as the Sunnis tell us. Listen," and he leans toward them over the edge of the pulpit, his voice husky.

"In the year 939 God concealed the twelfth *imam*. Allah hid him from the material world. And he never died at all. His concealment continues even today, and it will continue until Allah commands him to appear again on earth before the Last Judgment, to appear as the Mahdi." The *imam* radiates as he pronounces that word.

"And he will vanquish the enemies of the faithful and inaugurate an age of peace. And that is why we, the true Muslims, long for the hidden *imam*. We yearn for him as we yearn for Allah."

27

They say you bring the word of God,
yet all I hear is talk of good and bad ---
   nothing of love or truth.

Meanwhile, Rumi saunters beside Shams through the streets of Konya to attend a discourse by *imam* al-Farabi, whose followers are stirring discontent against the sultan, his disciple. On his left, a bed of violets bends low in blue robes like dervishes meditating.

As he and Shams sway together in silent harmony, they enter the *souk*, scattering a flock of chickens at their feet, as sunlight casts beams through rooftop openings onto piles of crimson pomegranates and standing sacks of white, brown, and black beans. They stroll past a row of weavers, who are pulling blue and green threads through their looms, mumbling as they tie knots again and again. Tufts of wool cover the floor from their carding. On the left, canaries, robins, and chickadees chirp and chatter in their wooden cages, some flapping their wings, others nestling in reed baskets, as feathers float in the dusty light. A sweet, pungent scent hangs in the air.

An old man selling apples and turnips spies Shams and curses under his breath. "Infidel!"

Two more merchants with cages holding lizards and ducks cover their faces and hiss, "You go against the law!"

Knives pierce Rumi's chest. *The law goes against the heart!*

Just then, a black-veiled woman, leaning on her husband's arm, which is loaded with silver trays, gathers up her skirts to avoid touching Shams as he passes.

His hairless brow furrowed, his jaw set, Shams growls, "Money is the *ka'aba* of those people, the direction of their prayers."

Rumi nods. "Kimiya is the *ka'aba* of Shahid." The dervishes chuckle.

"Power is the *ka'aba* of Aloeddin," Shams adds, a warning note in his voice.

"Yes, Velad will carry on the spiritual chain of the brotherhood. God the Exalted is the *ka'aba* of his heart."

They move out of the market and through an open grassy area. Arriving at *imam* al-Farabi's *medrasa*, Rumi and Shams pass through a courtyard into a small hall, where Brothers in brown robes sit on green carpets. A hanging ceramic lamp sheds light onto a corner of the room, where Shams takes a seat and beckons him to come over.

The *imam*, on an ornate pulpit with a one-eyed Koran reciter nearby, continues an ongoing sermon. "Last year, the infidels lost the holy land to us. Why were we victorious? Because God permitted a small force to vanquish a large one. Now, another infidel ruler is invading Egypt, seeking to conquer the believers of Allah. When our brothers question the true faith of the sultan, he throws them into prison! Where is his loyalty?"

Rumi bristles at the accusation.

Then, lifting his chin, the *imam* shouts, pounding the pulpit, "Brothers, let us unite, Arabs and Turks, in this *jihad*, a holy war against Christians and Mongols. Go and join the righteous martyrs and you will be on your way to paradise."

Shams is squirming while al-Farabi's students are nodding their heads and grunting their assent. Rumi strokes the hand of his beloved to calm him, but with each passing moment Shams' restlessness is more evident until he jumps to his feet.

"How much longer are you going to waste your time repeating words of war? You are like a parrot mouthing the angry phrases of others. The time is here for the inner war – the *jihad* against hatred."

The *imam*'s eyes bulge. He gulps in mid-sentence and marches out of the hall.

"And you," Shams accuses the students, "why are you studying to become like him? To make a good impression? To win your own *medrasa*? Knowledge is a rope. Its purpose is to lift you out of the pit, not help you climb into deeper pits. Fix your sights on knowing who you are, not on the letter of law."

The one-eyed Koran reciter turns his back on Shams and struts out the door. The other students parade out of the hall mumbling and shooting hostile glances at them.

In the empty room, he swivels toward Shams, seated again beside him. "My friend, as the Koran says, all you can do is be a reminder. Over them you have no power."

Shams embraces him with a silent, knowing glare. "I am your reminder, always."

But Rumi, not fully comforted, dreads the unforeseen consequences of this event. His lower lip trembling, he begins to pull the hair on his neck until the skin stings.

28

In this house of mirrors
you see a lot of things –
rub your eyes,
only you exist.

Omar, enraged at the violation of courtesy, strides across town to petition sultan Kaykobad to take action against Shams. Passing the bathhouse, he slows to catch his breath when a Christian merchant in a black robe and skullcap brushes his arm going the other way. Gasping, he covers his mouth and nose with his hands. *He defiles the air I breathe! I must rush to do ablutions!*

Racing through the palace gate and crossing the courtyard to the fountain, he splashes his nose and mouth with water, saying prayers under his breath. Agitated and impatient, he enters a smaller courtyard and joins the line of petitioners with their backs against a wall.

Finally at the front of the line, he receives permission to enter and climbs up to the great wooden door. Following a servant, he finds Sultan Karatay reclining on a gold-threaded cushion and counting piles of *dinars* on a tray with his tax collector. Without looking up, the ruler nods to him to speak.

"Sultan, this Shams of Tabriz is a troublemaker and a boaster, disrespecting *imam* al-Farabi, who lives in high esteem. Rumi was a prince but now, with that heretic at his side, he has become a lunatic."

The sultan raises his head and levels his eyes with his, nodding for him to continue. His sense of urgency rising, Omar exclaims, "You don't understand the danger here. Rumi and Shams are trying to initiate a new order with poetry and dance! They have turned their backs on the faith and ridicule its tenets. Shams even calls Rumi the second Mohammed!"

The sultan pushes the tray aside. "Omar, perhaps Shams' boasting is his intoxicated state. Others overpowered by God have made mad utterances. Perhaps. . ."

"Then he is a shallow vessel who overflows. And he should be punished for relinquishing the faith and for humiliating my *imam*!"

"I will consider your petition. Tell your *imam* to keep his followers under control, or they will be punished."

His shoulders sagging, Omar begins the trek back through town, knowing he has failed in his task to convince the ruler of the truth.

Since the Brothers learned the turn the month before, the Master appointed Shahid to assist Mehmet in making conical felt hats. They arranged to meet in a room with a hearth so that they can heat water.

Arriving first, Shahid places a long workbench in the center and brings in a large reed mat from the basket maker to cover the floor. Then he hangs a round pot full of water over the fire and tends the flames.

When Mehmet comes in, he chooses a sleek, silver knife, pulls a bunch of sheep's wool from an unruly pile, and begins to wash and comb it so that the fibers lie in the same direction. "It's going to form felt for the hats," he explains.

As Shahid watches, someone bangs on the door. It flies open and Omar towers on the threshold, swinging his fist through the air. "What do you think of that Shams -- and that turning. It's forbidden by the Koran!"

Shahid steps backward until his hand touches the cold wall, the one-eyed dervish's words pinning him against it.

"Yes, Shams is a troublemaker. He is so low – he would steal the shoes from a mosque!" Mehmet growls without looking up, as he uses the point of the knife to carve the wool into ovals and teases apart the fibers, until bits fall like snow onto the mat. "And Aloeddin thinks so too," he grunts.

"I know." Omar paces the room, his brown caftan flapping around his ankles, while Mehmet, with his fat hands, pats the soft, spongy ovals to an even thickness and tosses them onto the mat. "He is a member of those infidel Assassins, and you know what that means. When he has Rumi totally under his spell, he'll demand the unspeakable – that he jump to his death! We must stop this heresy before it's too late."

Mehmet rolls up the mat, ties it with a cord, and begins to kick the roll back and forth across the floor, slapping it with his feet. "We're going to get him -- like this!" the stodgy Brother shouts, kicking, until sweat pools under his arms and dribbles down his cheeks.

Shahid's knees buckle, and he lands on the floor.

With trembling hands, Mehmet unrolls the mat, peels off the flattened ovals, pairs them up, and joins two layers together with a sticky fluid until they become a seamless whole with a hollow center. Without glancing up, he places them into the steaming pot. When he removes them, the felt is stiff and thick. He picks an oval and, forming a fist, pushes the bottom end all the way up inside to meet the top. Then he places it over a wooden block and leaves it to dry.

"Like a tombstone," Omar mutters, pointing to the hollow hat. "*His* tombstone." Turning his back on them, he storms out of the room.

Mehmet places his thick hands on his hips and faces Shahid. "The time will come when you will have to choose sides."

Shahid wraps his arms around his knees and curls into a ball, whimpering, as Mehmet exits the room.

29

Even if you leave in anger
and stay away for a thousand years,
You will return to me
for I am your goal.

On the following day, as twilight settles on the reception area, the sunset call to prayer rings through the air. Aloeddin strides into the room to do prostrations, not knowing that his father is there. Rumi sits upright on the edge of a cushion, his shoulders back, his robe falling in folds over his legs, with *tesbih* beads in his open palm. His eyes, small slits, focus inward. Jami the cat purrs by his side.

Is this the eloquent teacher whose scholarly fatwas are known far and wide? Or is this an empty shell, vacant, spacious, and cold?

Shams enters just as Aloeddin is impatiently rushing out. The dervish pauses, twisting his head back toward him, his gaze unfocused, his glance suspended.

He protests, "Shams, it's the hour of prayer!"

"Aloeddin, the noise of your mind disturbs this holy place." Shams' eyes clear and pierce him. "Don't you understand the hidden meaning yet? The mosque is inside you. Union with Him *is* the essence of prayer."

Shams moves further into the room and takes a seat on a cushion opposite Rumi, folding his knees and placing his hands in his lap. As Aloeddin watches, he takes one breath and disappears into emptiness.

This is my *house. That intruder has no right to treat me in that way.*

Velad arrives and tries to enter the reception room. But he grabs his brother's sleeve, pulls him aside, and presses him, "Velad, who is this thief who has stolen our father, turning him into an intoxicated fool? Do you like what he has become?"

"This is the Sufi path, brother. Shams puts him through test after test, and with each ordeal, he loses something of his old self, entering a new world. Don't you see his ecstasy?"

"False ecstasy!" Aloeddin snarls, "He dances to music. He takes women disciples. He misses prayers because he's meditating. It's heresy!"

"Brother, there is nothing we can do now. It is in God's hands." Velad passes through the doorway.

"No!" *Just as the Prophet purged the* ka'aba *of its idols, so I will purge this house!*

The hearty scent of bread baking wafts toward him from down the hall, and his belly gurgles. He rushes toward the kitchen door but stops short in the doorway. The large copper pot, which always hung in the hearth, is gone, a silver kettle in its place. His eyes search the room frantically. The etched coconut cup, a gift from his grandmother to his mother, which sat beside the water jug, is gone, replaced by a green glass.

Kira comes toward him, offering a slice of bread. His mouth fills with juices, but his mind objects and he shakes his head. "No, I can't eat any longer from the hands of a convert."

30

Is there any place where the Sun doesn't shine?

Distressed by the rising acrimony toward Rumi, Sultan Karatay paces the length of his chamber, his white robe flapping against his legs as he reflects. Even in the early years, just after the time of the Prophet, Muslims fought among themselves. The Sunnis defended Uthman, the third caliph, as leader of the faith. And those others defended Ali, the son-in-law, and his son, the martyr Husayn. Even today, in his city, under his dominion, the Abode of Peace is split apart and the *sheikhs* fight among themselves.

The ruler surveys the gold-threaded brocades from Bursa that decorate his walls. He slows to stroke a fluffy bear fur on the divan and smiles at the pleasure of these distractions. His latest acquisition, a bow made of maple with a horsehair bowstring that is steeped in beeswax, rests against the wall. He will need to find one of those new pine arrows with a goat-bone tip and swan feathers so he can practice his shots. A knock interrupts his thoughts.

"Enter."

Emir Pervane crosses the threshold and bows. "My sultan, I have a proposition to bring together the Sufis. Let's sponsor a concert of music and dance so that members of the various orders can join in the festivities and soften to one another."

A solution to the conflict has presented itself. "Let it be done." He rubs his hands together in expectation. "I am ready to eat."

A eunuch slave arrives with a small table, which he sets beside the divan, as the scent of spiced mutton comes toward him.

On the evening of the *sema*, dervishes arrive in small groups, clustering around their *sheikhs* outside the hall and speaking under their breaths. Rumi slips out of his shoes and leaves them in a dark, leathery mound along the edge of the building. After filing in with Shams, he sees the Naqshbandis and Qadiris, along with Omar and his Brothers, standing off to the side with the other sober Muslims who refuse to participate in the dance.

Following the recitation of the Koran, the sultan, his gold earring shimmering, raises his index finger toward the musicians, and the first note of the reed-flute sings. The rubaab joins in, then the viol. A young boy plays wooden clappers. And the drummer beats his instrument with a stick. The heaviness lifts from Rumi's shoulders as the men lift their feet from the ground.

They whirl around the hall, their skirts unfolding, their arms outstretched, a flock of birds in perfect formation. Rumi joins the others, spinning in the dance that elevates them out of themselves, the dance that is prayer itself.

The sultan spins his red robe into the dance too. But a moment later, he loses his balance, his arms beat the air, and his skirt brushes against another – the skirt of Shams.

His friend's face darkens. Shams stamps his foot and halts among the whirlers. Another man halts, then another.

Rumi rushes over to him. *No man should ever touch another in the dance!* Taking Shams by the hand, he leads him out of the hall.

At the doorway, Shams turns his head back and sneers at the sultan, "He's not fit for the turn!" Then he bolts into the darkness. Rumi's heart leaps after him.

Appearing humiliated, the ruler signals to his guards to go catch the guilty man. Swords drawn, they dash into the night to find Shams.

Rushing out, Rumi climbs the hill in the darkness, shivering in the moist air. He listens for Shams' footsteps. He feels for his presence. But Shams has vanished into the mist.

Hearing the guards scrambling up the hill, he waits. One of them whispers, "There, over there!" and runs toward the sound, wielding his sword.

Rumi gasps. *Did they find him? Did they. . . .*

The guards remain still, apparently listening for movement. But the only reply is silence.

When they turn back down the hill, Rumi follows behind, invisible. At the *sema* hall, the sultan is waiting, stern-faced, his sword drawn. "Well? Did you capture him?"

The guards are quiet for a moment, three figures hardly visible against the blackness. Then a hoarse voice speaks, "The troublemaker is dead. He will not be back."

31

Beating your wings and feathers,
you broke free from this cage.
You have vanished from this world —
what need have you to tie your robe?

The sun, a fiery red, disappears behind the hills, shrouding Konya in darkness. For Rumi, the city becomes a desert, not an oasis. His home is stolen from him, gone with Shams. Day after day, he looks with longing toward the horizon where his beloved's silhouette might appear against the sky.

His life becomes a hymn of homesickness. His soul, a restless gazelle penned up in a cow stall. This separation, a yellow autumn of dead leaves. If Shams is in Damascus, then Damascus is home, the seat of beauty. If Shams is in Samarkand, then it is the only sanctuary.

A year and a half after Shams arrived, Rumi sits alone again in the dark, his green robe and turban tossed aside. He ignites a small taper, which casts an arc of light on the ceiling, hoping that dispelling the darkness will stop his turbulent mind. But unbidden images flood him like a storm: *Shams of Tabriz, the King of the Tavern, has handed you an eternal cup, and God in all His glory is pouring the wine.*

He gets up and paces the length of the room to clear his mind, but there is no shelter from the storm. *A fish wants to dive from dry land into the ocean when it hears the roaring waves. A falcon wants to return from the forest to the King's wrist when it hears the drum beating "return." A Sufi, shimmering with light, wants to dance like a sunbeam when darkness surrounds him.*

Images pour down. Pacing, no longer able to contain the flood, he surrenders and goes with it instead. As the thinking mind shuts

139

down, he folds his leg to contemplate the inner pictures as they arise. He holds an image gently, entering its mood, its landscape.

O how the Beloved fits inside my heart –
Like a thousand souls in one body,
a thousand harvests in one sheaf of wheat,
a thousand whirling heavens
*   in the eye of a needle.*

When he opens his mouth, verses flow out. He sits back on the cushion, breathless. Feeling strangely satisfied and wondering if the poetry will lessen his bewilderment, he abandons himself to the unnamable force.

Once you taste the wine of union,
*   what will be your faith?*
You'll tell everyone
*   that the ka'aba and the idol temple*
*   are one and the same.*

He gasps at his own words. Rumi, the Muslim scholar, is long gone. He no longer knows himself. He can no longer give discourses on dead teachings.

The man who believed poetry was a waste of time is taken over by it. The verses burn in him and press their way out, flaming out of his mouth.

I pick up a stick,
*   it becomes a lute in my hands.*
I make a mistake,
*   it turns out for the best.*
They say, do not travel during the holy month.
I set out – and find a priceless treasure.

Velad enters the room. "Why are you speaking in poetry, father? Aren't poets' words inspired by *jinn*?"

"These poems want to be written, they *must* be written. These images force their way out of me as a seed breaks through the shell and explodes into new life."

He leans against the wall. "The seed was timed to open by the light of the Sun. I am only a poet by the grace of Shams, the grace of God."

Rumi hurries past the mosque toward the horizon. He does not stop there because he cannot bear those Brothers speaking of petty things another moment.

As he approaches a stand of birch trees, two old women cackle while they knot rags to low-hanging branches. *If only I could believe that such a ritual would make my wish come true, I would do it. I would do anything!*

The face of Shams has become for him the face of God. As he hikes up the rolling hills, every fiber within him longs to see him. He yearns for the sharp clarity of that voice, the scent of musk coming around the corner, the tapping sound of his staff. Everything else is gone, finished – but this *himma*, this yearning for Him.

In one part of his mind, he knows that Shams is a doorway; he is not Him. But in another part, the face of Shams, the Sun, has melded into the face of Allah, the one Light.

Then he comes to a dead stop, facing the horizon. *Perhaps this is merely another human attachment. Perhaps I just adore Shams, that single-minded dervish. Perhaps I am as attached as any ordinary man.*

Yet without the presence of Shams, I cannot die to myself and become a drop in the ocean. He sits down in prickly grasses, leans back on his hands, and gazes up at the sky.

The presence of Shams – sitting on the rooftop, knee to knee, eye to eye. He is there now, in that moment, the sun rising behind the Sun, his white light spreading over the dogs roaming below, the women filling pots, the children playing with sticks.

With Shams, how easy it is to love! No wanting, no striving, no wishing for love to be different – but as it is, here, now, on the rooftop.

Rumi's breath stops. He is jolted back to the prickly grass. Back to the sunless sky.

141

Stretched out on the reception room floor, Rumi lies on his back, palms down, head facing Mecca, in the posture of death. With Velad crouching at his side, he clutches his son's hand. "Nothing left of me now but kindling."

He releases his son's hand, turns onto his side, and gets up. He trips across the threshold and wanders absentmindedly out into the courtyard.

Roaming past the shops of dervishes, Rumi ignores the efforts of small boys to bow to him, and follows a pack of hungry dogs, his appetite for Him driving him here and there, in pursuit of a whiff around every corner. A group of men disperses from a mosque and mill about, debating the fine points of a sermon. Rushing past, he bumps into one, stops for a moment to stare into his face, then brusquely moves on in the murky gloom.

The passerby shouts at him, "Master, it's me, Husamoddin. Why do you pass by without greeting me?"

Rumi looks back at the speaker but does not recognize the face of his disciple. He is lost in *fana*, intoxicated on the edge of madness.

Days later, when he crawls across the threshold of his house, his thorny beard unkempt, his filthy robe in shreds, his hair hanging beneath a loosened turban, Kira is disgusted: *a filthy, smelly, disheveled man in the guise of my husband!*

She finds Velad and sneers, "Every day he's more like that Shams. Now he even smells like him!"

32

Gardens, flames, nightingale,
* Whirling dance, and brotherhood –*
Throws all these away
* and throw yourself into His love.*

A yellow moon rises behind the minarets in a candlelit sky. Trembling, Rumi stands on the rooftop terrace, his head tilting up, his arms pleading with God. Everything that is spent in grief in him now concentrates itself into a powerful force.

My beloved lied: he said he would always be here.

God lied. He is too stunned to think it.

Betrayed by God? If everything is God's will, He cannot betray me.

Rumi recalls Job, the symbol of human endurance in the face of loss. And Jesus, the Christian prophet who felt forsaken on the cross. Perhaps his faith failed him too.

Faith – that certainty that God alone writes events and that he is part of His plan. He must not stop seeking God now out of fear of not finding Him. Otherwise, his destiny will become his enemy.

Exhausted, Rumi stumbles downstairs. People seem to rush at him. Their mouths are moving, but he cannot make out the muffled sounds all about him. Kira waves her arms. Kimiya stands behind her mother, confused and teary-eyed. Velad pushes a pile of documents toward him. Mehmet shouts something about new discourses.

Rumi shakes his head, wandering off in a daze. An abyss separates him from them now. That life has died, beheading his rationality. Now, he is drunk on the wine of Him, no longer on the edge of madness -- but over it.

He will go to the prayer lodge, far away from the noisy demands of the Order.

But the disciples find him and gather around him. Iqbal is about to ask a question when a peddler selling *halva* approaches and hands Rumi a small piece. As the sweetness crumbles onto his tongue, he tastes the one true taste. Turning his back on the Brothers, he silently follows the *halva* vendor down the street, longing for more delight.

"This too is the power of Shams!" Iqbal shouts behind him. "You are blinded by the sweetness and follow it mindlessly, even after it's gone."

The next afternoon a dervish brings startling news: he has seen Shams of Tabriz. Rumi begins to clap and shout. He races to the mosque in search of Velad and, on arriving, paces about, his hands buried in his tattered robe. Several gravel stones burrow into the bottoms of his sandals making his footstep painful, but he does not stop to remove them. Three boys skip by with burning torches to celebrate the end of the rainy season and the coming of the sun. But for Rumi, the Sun does not shine.

Velad comes out of the mosque, and he rushes toward him. "Son, you must leave tomorrow to reclaim Shams at any cost."

33

O blessed eyes!
I have seen something beyond imagination,
*   unreachable by fortune or human effort.*
I have seen the perfect face
*   of Shams of Tabriz*

Set to travel at night to avoid the sun's scorching arrows, Velad's small caravan prepares to leave Konya and head east. Sheep bleat, donkeys bray in the mist. A gray-bearded carpet maker in a baggy white tunic and pantaloons, his shoulders wrapped with a blue cloak, heaves one rug after another onto a brown mare. Others in caftans and turbans wave their arms about, giving directions to boys who load carts with supplies.

Wandering about, restless, Velad feels torn: he does not want to leave home on his father's errand, riding here and there without hope of success. Furthermore, his success will only bring more trouble.

I listen and obey, he sighs with resignation.

The troupe departs and, gradually, the continual thumping of horse hooves and cart wheels against the dirt overtakes the familiar sounds of Velad's life: his father's enchanting voice reciting the teachings, the shouts of merchants hawking wares in the bazaar, the chattering of green and yellow parakeets in the old bird market. Astride a pony, Velad cranes his neck and stares backwards until the silhouette of a single tapering minaret remains.

The caravan moves over rough hills like a lumbering, many-legged insect. Eventually, its bumping and swaying soothe him. The fields stretch away from him, whispering olive trees on one side, rustling grasses on the other. The animals, whose shapes he can make out against the horizon, carry peoples' loads on their shoulders, stopping to nibble when the caravan slows. The camels stick their small heads forward, wag their long, thin necks, and bounce their riders up and down on their humps.

Finally, near a rosy dawn, the party stops in a small valley surrounded by rocks that will block the day's sun. Quickly, a village of tents springs up. Men tend the animals, while women prepare small meals of unleavened bread, dates, and cheese.

At first light, with no tower in sight for a *muezzin* to make the call to prayer, a man stands on flat ground and sings out, "Come to prayer, come to the highest realization." The travelers abruptly stop their tasks, spread sand over their arms and faces, and face southwest toward Mecca. They bow and prostrate themselves, setting their foreheads on the dusty earth.

After a few hours of sleep and a meal, twilight brings the coolness, and the caravan leader calls out for departure. The troupe finds its rhythm in the creeping pace of the animals and foot travelers in the foggy mist. Swallows whirl overhead in undulating formations. Small bands of Turkmen nomads are setting up their wide-angled, black goat-hair tents in the shelter of olive groves. Women in brightly striped clothing light small, flickering fires that lick the air nearby.

As darkness spreads its wings over them, they roam up and down the dried, grassy hills. Rocked by the horse's motions, Velad digs into a small paper sack filled with sugar lumps and chews absent-mindedly. But the sugar does not satisfy him. A restless yearning stirs in him, like the restless wandering of the caravan here and there. It troubles him in a quiet way, not like the trouble of danger or loss, but like the trouble of separation from something he has only sensed, a grasping for something that cannot be grasped.

Velad and the others turn south toward Damascus, climbing barren, dusty hills. A sea of heat waves surges toward him, then the outline of a sprawling guesthouse rises from the endless plain. Eager for nourishment, he slides off his horse and greets the doorkeeper as he passes through huge wooden gates into the inn. Animals ramble beside him into a large open courtyard with a splashing fountain. His pony roams up and begins to slurp water as he dismounts.

The sun-blasted, earth-colored walls of the guesthouse climb up around him. Dark, winding staircases that lead to the roof intrigue him. But he is famished, and the sweet smell of spices causes him to salivate. He enters a large domed room where fires burn, making the walls gritty with soot. Small holes in the dome allow the smoke to leave and the fresh air to enter. A woman with a whimpering infant in a hammock on her back is spinning dough into the air, thinning it into flat bread. She places a piece onto an oblong stone and stoops to let it down into a fire, which spits and snaps.

As the scent of baking wheat wafts toward him, he reaches into his robe for coins, but the cook shakes his head. "The sultan provides the food. You are a guest at the inn."

Delighted, he returns to the courtyard to eat. Sour yogurt cools him down, and sweet rice fills his belly as he looks around. A foreign merchant in wide yellow trousers, green sash and long waistcoat, is sitting atop a bale of colored silks. Another stranger in a long white kilt and crimson velvet jacket is swaggering across the yard with a silver dagger in hand.

Just then a hostile current sweeps through the crowd, and heads turn toward a lone man who seems to give off a haughty aloofness as he treks from the gate to the cooking room. Velad has never observed anyone like him. From beneath his woven belt, crystal balls sway as he moves. A pendant of jade stones hangs from his neck. In one hand he carries a string of large wood prayer beads, the size of lemons.

"It's a disciple of Hajii Bektashi, who betrays the community of believers," a nearby traveler hisses.

"Those Bektashis are infidels disguised as Muslims!" another moans. "They drink alcohol and let women join in their practices." The irritated men shake their heads.

Velad's curiosity is aroused but, just as he is about to approach the men with his questions, his small band is assembling and exiting the wooden gates.

In Damascus two weeks later, Velad approaches yet another tavern in search of Shams of Tabriz. With heavy heart, bone weariness and a dry tongue, he scans the clusters of men huddling on wooden stools, their elbows resting on inlaid tabletops, the sleeves of their caftans falling to their knees, their voices chattering softly. A few are reading books lying open before them and sipping glasses of hot tea. A white-bearded elder in a soiled caftan leans against the wall and stares vacantly ahead. Two men pace the floor, their swords and daggers in plain sight. A dark restlessness fills the tavern.

There he is. Velad spies the object of his father's desire. His heart thumps as he remains still and watches from a corner. The sun casts a beam on Shams' clean-shaven head. His pointed hat rests at his feet, and his wooden staff leans against the table. The tiny lines above his beard have deepened into valleys. Small sacks have formed beneath his gray eyes. He sits opposite a stranger, a young Christian boy, perhaps sixteen years old, in threadbare brown robes with a cowl and a small white woolen cap. Both are concentrating on a chessboard as the prayer hour arrives.

The men rise, push back their stools and lift their many-colored rugs, which float to the ground. After raising their palms in unison and bowing, they prostrate toward Mecca.

Slower to find floor space, Velad notices that Shams' chess partner does not budge. As he kneels, the stranger coyly moves a piece on the board, drops his glance to the floor, and returns his hand to his lap. His prayers completed, Velad gets up.

Shams reseats himself, his eyes riveted on his partner. Without a flinch, the dervish reaches out and corrects the secret move. In the next moment, he calls out, "Sultan Velad, why do you hide from me? Come over here!"

Startled, Velad cautiously moves across the tavern toward Shams' table. He nods toward the monk, then bows, "Shams of Tabriz, *Asalaam alaykum.* I bring you a letter from my father begging you to return to Konya," and places a piece of parchment on the table.

The Christian monk, his head hanging, pushes the chair back and mutters, "Shams, please accept my apology for underestimating your wisdom and your rank. Let me repay you in coin."

"Francis, my brother, let this be past between us. You are young and not yet worthy of testing your powers against me. But someday you will be."

With the palm of his right hand, the dervish touches the man's head. "Return home to Assisi and fulfill your destiny. One day the birds will sing for you." With that, the Christian monk departs.

Shams swivels on his stool to address him. "Velad, are you another temptation in this tavern? I cannot return. My enemies are everywhere in Konya. Tell Rumi, he understands."

"No, Shams, he doesn't. Grief has torn him limb from limb. He has prepared the town. Your enemies are dispatched and you will be safe," he adds, placing a sack of gold coins on the table.

"He wants to buy me with gold?" The dervish lifts his staff and shoves the moneybag and the letter onto the floor. "Only his heart will do!" Then, looking intently into his eyes, the dervish bellows, (space)"I left him so that he would burn! So that he would face the final death of the self."

Cringing at the force of these words, Velad stoops to pick up the coins scattered across the floor. Standing again, he avoids the dervish's glare. "The money is for our trip back, Master. Shams, without the wick there is no flame."

The dervish's forehead furrows in a ridge above his hairless brows. He says nothing but cocks his head as if he hearing a faraway sound.

Velad fears all is lost and prepares to depart.

Just then, Shams straightens his head. "For Rumi I will come. So be it, as God wills, *insh'allah*."

Outside the tavern, Velad offers his horse to Shams and begins the long march beside him back to Konya. The moon glitters into her fullness two times before the travelers arrive at the inn of Zindjirli, a night's ride away from Konya, where they send a messenger ahead to announce their imminent arrival.

34

If someone asks,
"What does perfect beauty look like?"
show him your own face and say,
    Like this.

A year after Shams' disappearance, crowds gather around Rumi to accompany him toward the city gate. When he witnesses Shams rising from the horizon, sitting regally atop the horse, Rumi cannot contain himself but rushes forward with his arms open wide. In one swift motion, Shams slips off the horse and into his arms.

A reed-flute breaks into a gay melody, seeming to praise the resurrection of spring. Dancing around one another, clapping to the music, he cries joyfully, "You came! And this time you approached the city as a king, my Sun."

The sultan, tricked by his lying guards, executed them. But Rumi's grievous suffering led even him to welcome back the troublemaker. In tribute, he sent a dozen white candles to Rumi's *medrasa*, and Kimiya received them.

Now, as she lights one taper after another to prepare the reception area, she shudders, knowing that Rumi will disappear again and leave her mother sad and alone. She is aware that her mother dreads this moment, even though Kira publicly supports Shams' return. *After all, an obedient wife wants what her husband wants. An obedient wife prays that her husband's prayers are answered.*

But this prayer, this desire for Shams' return, means that her mother may lose Rumi again. This time, perhaps, forever.

151

Kimiya does not comprehend how Shams has captured Rumi's heart so that he cares about no one else. But, in stealing her father's heart, Shams also has stolen her mother's happiness. She lights the final wick, wondering what will become of them all.

Velad rushes into the candlelit room and takes a seat on the wall opposite his father. Rumi's restlessness has ceased. His folded legs are still, his hands nested in one another. His head has fallen to his breast, caressed by Shams' presence.

But a question at the back of Velad's mind prods him to speak. He turns to Shams and breaks the silence. "Master, the guards said they drew their knives and slashed you – yet you escaped."

Shams grunts. "Cheap trick! Inside my robe there is nothing but God."

35

You say he looks crazy –
That's only because your eyes are not tuned
to the music by which he dances.

At the mosque, Velad is standing beneath an arched portal surveying the city below, where the sultan's workers are scraping engraved images of saints off of a stone wall in order to convert a local church into a mosque. Someone clears his throat, intruding on his thoughts. Stepping back through the archway, he sees that his visitor is Iqbal. Rumi's son anticipates what he will hear.

"Velad, we need your help," the Brother pleads. "Don't you see what has become of your father since the arrival of that Shams? Don't you worry that this time he will not regain his senses?"

Velad nods. "Yes, Iqbal, father is with Shams again, fixed on his face. For him, everything else is void. But, thanks to him, his pain is eased. Can you be glad for him?"

Iqbal huffs, shuffling his feet. "Why does he need a human beloved? Why does our *sheikh*, who has reached such a high station, need another *sheikh*?"

Velad contemplates the question for a moment. "My father doesn't want to be the target of everyone's attention. He doesn't want to be lured into power or pride, so he offers another as his *sheikh* to us, surrendering to him and telling us to do the same."

"But Velad, why this rude, arrogant dervish?"

"Who can say why we love one person and not another?" Velad adjusts his turban and becomes thoughtful. "I believe father was not truly a Master until he became a slave of Shams."

36

Happy is the moment when we sit together,
with two forms, two faces, yet one soul,
you and I.

Shahid moves through the hills, where pomegranates have burst into red flowers, peaches into pink, and mint scents the air. But he does not see the miracle of spring. He focuses straight ahead, following Shams and Rumi, who stroll hand in hand, like shadow and body, toward the house of the goldsmith, Salaoddin, where they will take another retreat.

At times Rumi seems to be an ordinary man. But there is another life inside him too. Shahid can see it when the Brotherhood gathers, and he becomes larger, giving off a strange light. His speech changes too, becoming full of signs pointing to another world, and the power and beauty of his words seem to release something inside Shahid and to alter what he sees and smells and feels.

The face of the serious scholar hides this other face, which is turned inward, toward a well of such depth that his students cannot fathom it. Occasionally Shahid glimpses it, when Rumi rises from prayers and a fire blazes in his eyes. Or when he picks up a text and a word flashes from his tongue.

I fear for the Master as those moments. I wonder if that other invisible life will rise out of him, a hungry beast, and take his ordinary life into its mouth, devouring it like a piece of meat.

Roused from his thoughts, Shahid watches as Shams pulls Rumi inside the house and closes the door once more for forty days and forty nights. A dark veil comes down over Shahid's world. Dimly, he recalls his father walking off with his brother in the same way, pulling him by the arm, taking him all for himself. They turn their backs on Shahid and move toward a caravan, leaving him standing there alone, as always.

A single candle illuminates the darkness in the small, spare room. A prayer mat and a clay jug of water are its only furnishings. Rumi sits on a pillow face to face with his beloved. Those eyes, bottomless pools. The candle sputters. The cushion disappears beneath him. He dissolves, lake water rising into mist.

But all too quickly his mind grabs the fear, and the self solidifies again, becoming ice. He can taste *fana*, but he cannot establish it as a permanent station.

I could hold on, protect myself. Or I could enter this new world, and die.

Shams whispers up close to his face, "Your way begins on the other side of the wall. Walk out into open space."

A snake's black head rears up inside Rumi's mind. Her yellow eyes seduce, her tongue darts. Her lower body coils against the ground at his feet, her upper body lifts toward his face, closer. *Hiss.*

She circles around his breast and wraps herself about him, tighter. He squirms against the grip. But she tightens it and slides slowly down his torso, winding around his legs.

Nafs! Images flash before him, dark and jarring reflections of himself: a young man standing at his father's pulpit, the community of believers revering him, attempting to make of him an idol. And a part of him permits it, even enjoys it – pride!

And that demon never left me. I know more, I am more than the others. When I play humble Sufi, the demon only coils more deeply into my belly, waiting to strike.

"Pride betrays you like the onions you eat," he hears Shams say. "Breathe and let it go. Turn your heart in repentance."

The pride goes out with his breath, deflating his chest and sweetening the taste in his mouth. His head falls forward. The unconditional quality of Shams' love encircles him and permits the demons to return to the light.

A new image comes up: the boy stands at the threshold of his home, the knocking of his mother's kitchen pots behind him, the sight of his father's back moving away before him toward the mosque. He wants his father's piety and power for himself -- envy!

Then that moment, on the street of the mirror sellers, when he first sees Shams – and wants *his* freedom, *his* fierceness, *his* trust in Allah.

A sharp pain stabs at his chest. He inhales, filling his chest until the pain eases, imagining the envy dissolve as air meets air.

Turning his heart in repentance, soon he can watch the *nafs* like any other thoughts rising and falling. The snake lifts her head and slowly unwraps herself from his body. Then, uncoiling from the ground, she winds her way toward the door.

Rumi relaxes, once again aware only of those untamed eyes. In Shams' presence, he moves into the present, no past pulling on him, no future calling to him. Only the perfect beauty of this instant.

After a while he feels no need to hold onto time, to imprint events in any way, because the next moment and the next are just as full and deep as a well to quench his thirst.

And then even these moments disappear because *he* disappears, annihilated in union with him, his *sheikh*, his doorway. Living in the scholar's river of time, he was constantly aware of time passing and of rushing to keep up, to make a mark so that something of him would remain. But with Shams, living in presence, each day, no, each moment, is a clean slate – nothing remains.

One afternoon Salaoddin's daughter shuffles past the room where Rumi and Shams remain in retreat. The door is ajar. She glimpses Rumi kneeling before a tub of water, head bowed. He is tenderly washing Shams' feet.

No one is permitted to enter the retreat except Jami, Rumi's cat. When the men fast, Jami refuses food. Within weeks his gray fur thins and reveals a puzzle of bones.

When the men eat, Jami chews scraps from Rumi's fingertips. The cat licks his lips until flesh grows back on his bones and eventually pushes the gray fur out farther and farther. Once again, his mass becomes round and fuzzy, his movement slows, and his bones disappear beneath the hair. Rumi lifts him from beneath the belly and sets him, purring, onto his lap while he meditates.

37

Open your arms if you want
the Beloved's embrace.

Sleepers lie on rooftops across Konya, stretched out under the glimmering stars, dreaming of Rumi's discourses or Mongol invaders or feasts of *halva*. Kira lies on her mat, still as a tomb, and stares at the wall. Her husband has left her again for that dervish, and his departure seems to accuse her of something. *Of failure.*

A strange melancholy invades her body. She enters a world in which any pinpoint of light is instantly swallowed by the dark. She wanders through lightless, empty rooms, long corridors whose walls cannot be seen, only touched.

I will not give in to the darkness. I want Rumi back. Back in my kitchen, in my arms. Back without Shams, God willing.

She longs for the face of her husband, to hold it in her hands, to stroke his fuzzy beard, to lose herself in his dark wells. She has strived as a convert to follow the law as well as born believers. She has testified to the unity of God, performed ritual prayers, given alms to the poor. She has fasted on Ramadan.

But now, on her back, her legs down, her arms stretching out of her sides, she is drawn back to that small church in Ephesus, its steeple rising to the sky in a single point. There, she sits on the hard pew. She regards the simple wooden cross reaching out in all directions. Rubbing her thumb on her fingertips, she feels the round rosary beads and whispers to herself, "Our Father. . . Our Father, who art in heaven. . . ."

Kira recalls her favorite Bible story. Abraham, no, Ibrahim, as it is written, was willing to sacrifice his son, Isaac, in total obedience to God. *Now I must sacrifice my most precious attachment. After all, believers say that to become a Muslim you must lose what is most precious to you.*

When a soft glow pierces the night, Kira has no reason to rise. She lies on her left side, curling up tightly, when curiosity grips her. She wants to know what those two men do in that retreat day after day. *I need to know my husband's secrets!*

Hours later, the question persists. Her curiosity rises to such a pitch that she calls Sepahsalar to accompany her to Salaoddin's house. He waits outside while she receives permission to enter and passes through the reception room, where the goldsmith's bowls, buckles, earrings, and buttons are arranged in neat rows. She heads toward the spare room and stoops down to peek through a crack in the door.

The two men sit in silence, Rumi's back erect, his turban at his side. His face seems to radiate. She cannot tell whether it is from the light coming through the window.

Suddenly, an opening appears in the back wall of the room and three odd, misty-looking men in shiny green robes step through it. Thin and filmy at first, the strangers gradually take on form and substance. Their collarless, long-sleeved green mantles shimmer. They greet Rumi and Shams with their hands on their chests and place a bouquet of fresh flowers on the floor before them.

When the twilight fades outside, it seems to Kira to move indoors, casting a yellow glow around the men. The green-cloaked visitors signal to Shams to lead the sunset prayer, but he declines. They signal to Rumi. As her husband speaks the sacred words, the air around him sparkles. When he finishes, the three strangers turn and silently pass back through the wall as darkness creeps in.

Breathless, Kira slips away to the cooking area. The sunset prayer still moves within her, bringing calm, but the appearance of these other-worldly visitors disturbs her deeply. *Why do they seek my husband? What will become of him after all these strange events?*

Rumi emerges from the room and comes toward her without expressing surprise at her presence. Handing her the bouquet of flowers, he says, "Take care of these, Kira. Spiritual beings who tend paradise brought them as a gift to you. Do not reveal the secret of their visitation."

I have evidence in my hands! Evidence of God's intercession in our lives.

Back home in her room, the flowers beside her, Kira feels more alone than ever before. Her husband is now a man who wants for nothing and needs nothing from her.

Yet, somehow, she feels less lonely too.

I am Rumi's companion on this journey, and although it is more precious to him than I am, through him I am a part of something larger than both of us.

38

In the garden of your love
all I see are the flowers in bloom.
Could I ever turn toward the thorns?

Forty days later, lover and beloved prepare to leave *sohbet* again. They sit for the final few minutes in silence. Rumi observes the spider's web of lines on Shams' cheeks. He feels that they move now in one liquid medium, whose slightest movements ripple through them both without barriers.

His friend breaks the silence. "This friendship, like prayer, is conversation with the Holy One. I don't know if my soul is in your body or yours is in mine."

They get up and step down the stairs to the goldsmith's reception room, where crowds of people mill about, awaiting the Master. Some come hoping to embrace their *sheikh* again, while others come needing to let off the steam of anger caused by his second absence.

"Rumi, Shams, welcome back," says Husamoddin, grinning, as he bends his knee to kiss the hand of first one *sheikh*, then the other.

"Master," Iqbal inserts himself and demands, "what do you talk about in there?"

"Yes, what do you do with each other in secret?" another man quizzes with insinuation.

Rumi gestures to Shams to respond. But the dervish shakes his head. "The eye cannot peer directly at the Sun, but it can see the moon. Your words will make them understand."

"Brothers and sisters," Rumi begins, "I'm not who you think I am. I'm not part of a group that loves music or *sema*. I don't care about being famous, keeping the law, or breaking the law."

For a moment, he pulls at the beard on his cheek. "Love is my way to God. This friendship, this spiritual conversation, is my path."

To Shahid, Rumi seems taller now. His head floats on his neck like a flute stretches through his spine, and he hardly seems to touch the ground. His skin is translucent, and his pupils shine like flint in sunlight. But his words cause a shudder to pulse through the room.

39

While you look for love here and there,
the fire I lit inside you
will only grow cold.

Rumi folds his knees on the reception room carpet and closes his eyes to contemplate how to make it safe for Shams to remain in Konya. As his breath drops into his belly and his mind grows still, an image rises up: Shams, a gnarly cypress, beside Kimiya, a perfect, pink rose.

Returning his attention to the room, he sees that his friend has entered, taken another cushion, and is preparing to turn within. "Shams," he says gently, "I want to offer you the hand of Kimiya in marriage."

The dervish's brow creases in protest, but before he can utter a word, Rumi interjects, "My friend, let me finish. She will live with you, so you can stay legitimately in Konya. She will care for your needs, so you will be satisfied here. And, God willing, she will come to love you in time."

Rumi tips his head in thought. "Your age difference doesn't matter. Look at the Prophet and his youngest wife, Aisha. She could have been his grandchild, yet she became for him the lure to God."

"My friend, I don't need a lure to God."

He hesitates. "But Shams, this union will end the animosity in the minds of our enemies."

In response, the dervish's eyes seem to pierce him. "Rumi, my love for her will never be like our love, the meeting of two oceans. But I can see the light of Allah in her face and will accept her as my wife."

40

*The desire to know your own soul
will end all other desires.*

Placing crumbling chunks of *halva* onto a tray, Kimiya feels nostalgic for her lost childhood, when she ate as much *halva* as she desired while sitting on Kira's lap. She recalls those harmonious days when Velad and Aloeddin played together and Rumi stayed at home contented with the family. Of course, that was before he met Shams and became preoccupied with their spiritual conversation, causing Kira great distress. Before her brothers took sides and became adversaries in their father's love. Before she felt heavy and had to monitor how much *halva* she ate. Before she knew that her wishes would not come true. That her own father and mother had never died of the fevers. That Shams had never arrived in Konya.

Suddenly aware that her thoughts are improper and selfish, she shakes her head to quiet them. *God forgive me*, she pleads. *God forgive me!* And she fixes her attention on the work at hand, setting a small pile of wrinkled brown dates next to the *halva*.

Just then, her mother enters the kitchen, pauses, and looks at her sadly, as if in farewell. "What is it, mother? Are you all right?"

Kira's eyes drop to the floor for an instant, then return to meet hers. "Kimiya, Rumi has found a husband for you. Remember now, he's your father. You will obey."

Her heart stops. Staring at her mother, she searches for answers. The moment seems to extend indefinitely. Then the door of her mind snaps open – "Oh, no, mother, not. . . ."

"Yes, Kimiya. He gives you his own beloved."

Kimiya does not remember falling to the floor, but now she feels it cold and hard against her legs as a puddle of water seeps through her robe. Improper questions race through her mind again. *Why are other women content with arranged marriages and laws that forbid them to leave the house? And not I?*

She can no longer remember the faces of her parents. She can no longer feel the emptiness of their absence. Certainly, she can no longer recall sobbing to God, "If you are the most merciful, how could you have taken them from me?" But this loss sewed the seeds of an obscure doubt in her heart. And there they ripened to maturity, blooming into red, immodest questions.

A few minutes later, Kimiya wanders to the rear of the house, oblivious of the damp cloth sticking to her upper thigh. She leans forward and peeks through a hole in the back wall of the women's quarters, through which she can see the yard.

Shahid is by the well, his head bowed low. But his eyes wander up stealthily. Her breath catches in her throat. She doesn't need water just then, but she needs something else. Urgently. Without thinking, she goes to the kitchen, picks up the pitcher, and moves out the rear door toward the well.

Fixing her glance on the dirt even when she reaches the well, Kimiya places her jug down on the rim and attaches it to a rope. She lets out the rope, lowers the pitcher until it is filled, then draws it up with water.

He is leaning toward her, whispering. Her stomach fluttering, she cannot quite make out the words. She takes a step closer, continuing to pin her sight down. He tries again, and she barely hears, "You are my hidden treasure."

In the next moment, a long, brown hand reaches past her robe, brushing it slightly -- and she startles. *I must rush to perform ablutions!*

The hand sets a small jewel box on the rim of the well. Unable to resist, she swallows hard, snaps it up in her gown, whirls around, and rushes back toward the house. Dashing into the women's quarters, her knees buckle beneath her as she clutches the box. Then, coming to her senses, she pushes it under her sleeping mat, where it will lie hidden with her other dreams.

Reclining on her back, she stares up at the ceiling. She has broken the sacred law, disgracing her parents. *In another family I would be killed for dishonoring them.*

Following the dawn prayer, Kira shakes out the carpets. She knows there is no arguing with her husband. He is accustomed to being obeyed, and he will be obeyed in this marriage arrangement too. Fortunately, her earlier doubts about Shams' intentions and his spiritual station have lessened. Since witnessing the miracle of the flowers, she knows that this all-consuming fire between her husband and the dervish is not of this world. And although her mind reels at the thought of her sweet, innocent Kimiya with that gruff old dervish, she can accept it now.

Perhaps Kimiya's tenderness will reach into Shams and soften his harsh ways.

Kira piles the carpets in a corner of the reception area. An unfamiliar wall of silence separates her from Kimiya, who is using a cloth to clean the copper oil lamp.

The girl sighs. *I will go to my grave with my questions unasked—and unanswered. I am a pawn on my father's chessboard.*

169

41

I'm in love:

  All your advice – what's the use?

I've drunk poison:

  All your sugar – what's the use?

Alone in his cell, his throat parched, Shahid tries to reach for a water pitcher. But he feels such a jarring dislocation that he cannot find the ground beneath his feet. It yawns open into blackness. And the air! It is filled with the whirring of gnats whose relentless buzz give him no rest.

He sags onto the floor in a heap. Dry heaves arise from him as pain tightens his face.

Ever since he heard the news of Kimiya's marriage to that dervish, he has been unable to rise. *I will not attend the wedding. I will not participate in this sacrilege, even as a silent witness.*

Tentatively, he considers the questions that have been hovering at the cliff of awareness for days. *How could Rumi do this to his own daughter? Rumi, whose kindness and ability to see into others' hearts is renowned?*

And if Rumi did not do it, then who? A mad man who has taken possession of him and forced Kimiya to submit to that infidel?

But if Rumi did make this deal with the devil. . . Shahid stops. He cannot think it. He cannot follow the supposition to its logical conclusion. Lying down, he begins to whisper the name of God, the One who is the help in peril.

He tries desperately to comfort himself. But the dreaded thought finally intrudes: *If Rumi made this bargain, then I am lost, for I have given my oath to a hypocrite.*

When he awakens under the cloak of night, he feels terribly alone. Leaning on one side, he reaches under the carpet for his mother's Koran. He sweeps his hand across the floor but finds no book, no sign of his mother's gift.

The evening before becoming a wife, Kimiya tosses and turns on her sleeping mat, unable to find a comfortable place that fits her bones and curves. The man who is becoming her husband mystifies her. His intensity attracts her, yet terrifies her. His unwillingness to follow the sacred law of *Shari'a* draws her to him, yet repulses her at the same time. *Perhaps he will teach me about his secret ways. Perhaps. . . . she closes her fist. The sensation of those teats stiff with milk remains in her fingers.

Lying on her side with her knees drawn up, she falls into a tunnel of darkness, dreaming that the folds of her robes are twisted up in someone else's robes, entwining around her more and more tightly until she can hardly move. She throws her head around frantically and, freeing it from the folds, looks up to see. . . Shahid! He is lost in the tumble of fabric, scrambling up her body to reach her face, her lips. . . .

She screams herself awake, startled, flushed, ashamed. And sleeps no more.

At the call to prayer, she hesitates for a moment. *Perhaps I should pretend illness. No, that would call attention to me.*

Getting up, she smoothes her robe, pulls her headscarf tight, checking for loose strands of hair, and goes to join the women. Swinging her prayer carpet in front of her with a mechanical motion, she tries to shrink away from the others, to be unseen.

42

The lover's heart
is filled with an ocean,
and in its rolling waves
the cosmos gently turns.

In the reception room the next afternoon, Aloeddin looks longingly at a silver tray full of honeycomb beside a bouquet of yellow roses. About twenty guests recline on cushions or mingle about in the candlelight, awaiting the wedding ceremony and feast. Velad, Husamoddin, and Salaoddin huddle together in a corner, their turbans bobbing. Standing alone, in a pink frock, Kimiya appears like a lost child among the guests and musicians.

Rumi and Shams stand in the center holding hands. Aloeddin wants to demand, *whose nuptials are really taking place here?* But the question dies on his tongue.

Initiating the ritual, Rumi lifts his arms for the guests to rise. Behind his father, his fists clenched at his sides, Aloeddin is fuming. *This match means that Shams will stay in Konya. In my house. With my father.* Chewing on his upper lip, he tastes the salt of blood. Swallowing blood – a forbidden act! He dashes out of the room to wash his mouth.

When he reenters, his father is quoting the Koran. "Allah created mates for you from among yourselves so that you may live in tranquility with them. And He has put love and mercy between your hearts."

The groom and the bride's father sign the wedding contract as the women trill. Shams moves with formality to Kimiya's side but does not turn to face her. He signals for the festivities to begin. The drums take up a beat and the reed-flute joins in.

In their bedroom after the wedding, a single taper casts a circular shadow on the sleeping mat. Kimiya sits on the rug, her husband pacing before her. "Kimiya, your name means spiritual alchemy. We will live together in the heat of the furnace, turning copper into gold."

She does not hear the words as much as the harsh tone in her husband's voice, which carries a threat to her ear.

He continues, "When Allah created the earth, he separated men and women. Crossing the frontier only leads to confusion and unhappiness. Like my mother and yours, you will be happy in the women's quarters with Kira."

She wants to comply. She wishes she could cede the landscape of her inner world to her father's choice of husband. But, as he speaks, she thinks she can hear the strange guttural sounds of foreigners just outside the door. She wonders if they are fair-haired knights in coats of silver mail galloping through town. Shams' voice fades, and the imaginary sounds carry her away, outside the city gates, where the desert stretches in freedom, and oases of shady palms and sugary dates await her.

Sweeping his arm across the sights in the room, Shams says, "Everything you need is right here, my red flower. What more do you want?"

Her husband's question jolts her back to the dusky room, and she knows then that she was only dreaming. The frontier is within her, written on her very bones, and she will never cross it. She will accept the laws of her marriage as a binding decree. *I must submit. I must.*

43

If I were the plaything of every thought
I'd be a fool, not a wise man.
If the soul's light had to stay inside its house
I'd open every door and window.

Two weeks later, the mid-winter sun shines brightly on patches of melting snow, and Kira and Sepahsalar prepare to leave the house for a stroll in the vineyards of Meram. Kimiya watches as they put on their robes, and warring feelings compel her to speak. "Please, Mother, may I come with you?"

"But you are forbidden, child. Will you disobey your husband? I advise you not to come."

Kimiya's waking mind agrees with her mother, but some other part of it, a dark undercurrent, does not. She *wants* to go out into the world for a walk. She *wants* to see life outside her house and, as the possibility arises, she trembles with excitement. "Just this once. Please."

Her mother draws a breath. "Kimiya, I discourage you from going." She hesitates, looking away. "But I won't stop you."

With excitement and anticipation, she tucks her hair more firmly under the *hijab* and straightens her robes. Sepahsalar throws her a disapproving glance as he exits the front door and, for a moment, her excitement is chilled. Crossing the threshold, she sets foot outside, the direct light of day striking her face. Pulling the edges of her scarf down, she grabs Kira's hand as they leave the courtyard and step onto the dusty road.

Looking down at her feet as she walks, she avoids seeing what should not be seen. She knows this risky act is a sin, but at this moment her yearnings for the world are stronger than her fear of

God. For as long as she can remember, she has suffered these warring impulses. This outing might be her only chance to see the flocks of sheep roaming freely on the hillsides and to touch the green vines growing the fruit of forbidden wine.

Sepahsalar guides them off the main road into a small alleyway. She keeps glancing back over her shoulder to see whether anyone is following, whether anyone witnesses her departure.

As they pass a mosque with its towering minarets, her mother points out a small white church nearby, its single steeple rising into the sky. "St. Paul visited that church many years ago."

Curiosity bubbles up in her. "What makes a person Christian, Mother?" She forgets for a moment to look behind her.

"They believe in three Gods: the Father, the Son, and the Holy Ghost. But they don't yet accept the Prophet Mohammed, blessed be He."

Her mind stops. *Living without Allah or His Prophet or the holy book!*

"They believe in the crucifixion of Christ, which the Koran claims never happened," Kira continues. "And they don't get circumcised!"

Kimiya feels so confused that, for a moment, she forgets her fears and focuses instead on the sights. They are proceeding through a Jewish quarter, where cobblers stoop among piles of leather, and a few olive-skinned men with black caps go in and out of shops, their Spanish dialect clanging in her ears. Straining to understand what the merchants might be saying, she thinks she makes out, "those sons of Ishmael. . ." and quivers.

"These Jews, what do they believe?" she asks Sepahasalar.

"Their stores are closed on Saturdays so they can worship and drink wine. But there are people who are even stranger," he continues. "Velad told me that only thirty miles south of here men used to worship a female deity, a mother Goddess! They actually thought God was a woman. I take refuge in God from Satan," he bristles.

Shivers go up Kimiya's spine. *A female God. Would She have feelings and desires like mine too? Would She have answers to my questions?*

As they climb several hilly knolls, leaving the city behind, Kimiya can see row after row of the short, leafy plants that will yield purple grapes. The women descend onto flat grounds and Sepahsalar stands aside, while they hike the neat rows in silence, breathing the fresh air. Kimiya feels the warmth of the sun's rays penetrating her woolen robe until her skin begins to prickle from the heat. She removes her slippers and, when her bare feet touch the soil, a sensuous thrill courses through her.

Fluffy white clouds drape across far-off peaks, and Kimiya is overcome by the desire to lie on her back and watch them float away. She goes a short distance from the vineyards and stretches out on the earth, her *hijab* slipping back and strands of hair falling to her shoulders. Her ears feel bare and cool air caresses the top of her head.

Sepahsalar moves toward her and interrupts her happiness. "Evening prayers approach. We must return before the others, God willing."

The women reach the house before the men arrive and go directly to the kitchen to begin their tasks. Kimiya sets out salt, bread, yogurt and dried fruits. She piles a tray high with pomegranates and fills a pot to boil bulgur wheat. But, although she goes through the motions, she has not fully returned to the house. Still moving among the sheep and listening to their soft bleating, she feels the prickly carpet of grasses on the soles of her feet and the flush of the sun's heat beneath her clothes.

She is awakened from her reveries by the tapping of Shams' staff and the soft thumping of Rumi and Velad's footsteps as they enter the sitting room. She returns to stirring, smelling nothing now but boiling wheat.

Entering the kitchen, Shams nods toward her and asks her to pour him a glass of water. She feels his stare from across the room. It falls onto the hem of her robe and his eyes grow wide with alarm. Striding up to her, he bends over and picks something off her skirt.

Rising to his full height, Shams holds a dried, twisted twig between his thumb and forefinger and examines it like an unknown object. He looks at her with disbelief and back again at the leaf.

"You left the house." He lifts his staff and bangs it on the floor. "Come with me!" he demands, turning and marching out of the kitchen.

Together inside their room, he indicates for her to sit by pointing to the mat and stands over her. The purple veins on his hairless forehead throb. "What demon led you to disobey me?"

She feels his rage as the wrath of God Himself. Her body tightens, her eyes brim. Her bold will is far away now, her head in her hands. "I have sinned. May God, the all-forgiving, have mercy on me. May you find it in your heart to pardon me."

Pacing like a caged animal, Shams circles the room and steps over her body again and again. Flinching, she shields her head with her arms, too scared to peer up at him, afraid that with one foot he might crush her, or with that staff he might touch her and turn her into . . .*what?*

Suddenly, he stops. The silence is unbearable. "My desire for a proper marriage means nothing to you. Your action means my shame. I will have a divorce." With that, he parts, leaving the curtain swinging behind him.

Kimiya is struck dumb. *A banished wife! No other man to be my guardian.* Terrified, she curls up and rocks and rocks. "God forgive me, God forgive me."

She lies down, whispering her prayer. As the night darkens, a wave of heat comes upon her as if the sun's rays scorch her naked skin.

44

Silent like the earth,
my cries can be heard
beyond the turning of the Great Wheel.

Kira hears Shams storm off and, after completing a few chores, moves toward the bedroom to check on her daughter. Kimiya is rocking and moaning, her face wet with sweat, her eyes glassy. Kira runs over to her, helps her to lie back, and covers her with a blanket.

"Just rest, Kimiya, I'll get some honey water."

After putting on the water to boil, she goes through the house filling small pots with herbs and lighting them, until the air is scented with bitter fumes. Then she rushes about telling others to begin to pray for Kimiya's recovery. Soon, family members and neighbors gather in the reception area, and their droning pleas circle inside the four walls like birds unable to escape to the skies.

Returning to her daughter's side, Kira touches her cheek, as hot as a copper brazier. Her skin is thinning to parchment, and beneath it rivers of blood boil.

She hurries outdoors, soaks a cloth in the freezing snow, and returns to lay it on her daughter's brow. But the fluid evaporates in seconds. She lifts the girl's head and pours honey water onto the white, cracked lips, but it spills out the sides in rivulets. She fans her own hand back and forth, back and forth, over Kimiya's face to make a breeze, until she can no longer move a muscle from exhaustion.

Then a wintry ice invades Kimiya's body and every muscle clenches. Her fingers become rigid, her jaw tightens. Her skin contracts against the bone, and her lips emit the whine of a stray cat.

Trembling, Kira regains her focus and places another blanket over Kimiya. She sits and stares at the frozen girl, willing her back to life with every bit of force she can muster.

Again, huge beads of sweat break out on Kimiya's brow and drip down onto her hair. Her muscles loosen, her pores open to the air. Her blood boils and freezes, boils and freezes. Moaning, she drifts in and out of consciousness.

"*Husband!*" she shrieks, her right hand suddenly reaching out of the blankets into space.

Stunned, Kira stumbles to her feet and backs away from her daughter. *Shams – did he bring this about somehow? Is he using his magic to punish her, to maintain his own honor?* Kira's heart pinches tight in her chest, her own part in this series of events all too painful.

She rushes toward her daughter again, wrapping her arms around her and clinging to her desperately. She lets her head down on the girl's belly, where it bobs with each breath, and remains there all night in silence.

The next morning, Kira awakens in the darkness. Her head is not bobbing up and down. Kimiya is perfectly still, her honey-colored hair dry and matted around her face, her translucent skin the color of ash. Kira gasps and lets out a sob.

She hears Aloeddin, just beyond the curtain, his hoarse cry tearing through the house. "The poor girl dies of grief. Who could bear this Shams, this infidel?"

Pressing her hands to her ears, Kira wants desperately to get away, to be alone with her sorrow and her God, to say the prayer for the dead. But her mouth is shut tight, and her mind roars instead.

How could such a fever take her daughter so quickly? Could the fires of a husband's rage light the fires of a deathly fever in a young wife's body? Or was there some phantom already living in Kimiya's body that made her susceptible to igniting? And when the two touched – the outer fires and the inner flame – they burst into a conflagration, turning the girl whose name was alchemy into ash.

Unable to remain in the room of death, Kira finds her way into her own bedroom, lies face down on the floor, and sobs until the mat is soaked. Her heart pounds. It was she who allowed her daughter to take the forbidden walk. She participated in breaking Shams' rule. *God forgive me, the pain is too great to bear. God forgive me, I was only. . . .* Like her daughter, she too hoped to see more of life. Like her, she hated to be constrained by the laws of the *Shar'ia* in her first marriage. She too was angry at Shams and secretly wanted to get back at him, to hurt him for stealing Rumi.

And now Kimiya is gone. Rumi has retreated to the rooftop terrace. And she is alone with her grief, trying to see God's will in this event. She strives to see His hand in this event as more than punishment, more than retribution. Perhaps this loss can somehow become a sacrifice, a meaningful death, so that Kimiya can go to paradise, so that she, her mother, can survive this loss.

Kira struggles to conjure up Kimiya as an innocent, a daughter of God who gave her life in submission to her father's will. Her life, a testament to her faith. In this way, Kimiya's death can be made sacred.

45

A star has exploded in my heart
and the seven skies are lost in it.

Outside of Rumi's courtyard, a milky dawn appears. Shahid has paced throughout the night until the soft ground formed burrows beneath his feet. He has not tried to receive permission to enter. Just as he did not want an image of her wedding in his mind, he does not want to see Kimiya at her death. He wants only to remember her that first night, at the evening meal, when she bent and rose over the tray, her hands small and delicate, her cheeks like silk pillows, her eyes modestly avoiding him. His purpose, suddenly clear.

Now, without her, he cannot envision the next day and the next. *Praying, eating, making hats, praying, eating, sleep.* Only sleep will give him respite, the promise of oblivion.

Shahid falls to his knees and lets out a terrifying howl.

Shams stares at the empty mat where Kimiya was stretched out, lifeless. His fingers gently touch the dampness, her fluids. He dives within, trying to understand what happened.

He wanted her obedience, not *this.* He wanted a divorce, not death. Yet Kimiya is gone, her petals fallen.

As Shams tries to rise, his body is unsteady, weighty with grief. He uses his staff to push himself up off the ground. Once upright, he glances back at the death mat, turns, and leaves.

Outside, he extends one foot before the other without thought, without direction, first dirt beneath his feet, then cobblestone, then wild grasses that reach as high as his knees. One foot before the other, as darkness covers him, and stars blink into view. He lies down, the firmament his roof.

46

All of your sorrow exists for one reason –
that you may end sorrow forever.

Keeping himself awake by standing upright, Rumi remains alone on the rooftop terrace fervently saying the prayer for the dead. His eyes burn as he yanks a strand of hair under his chin.

At his moments of greatest exhaustion, the question he dreads most slips in between the repetitions of his prayer. *Kimiya's death, was it God's will or my own?*

He had a hand in it. Only two weeks earlier, he commanded her to marry Shams. *Did I make the match for my own ends?* It seemed a simple intention, to keep both Shams and Kimiya nearby, to give them both good company.

No, that is not the truth. His aim had been to keep Shams near him. He had not really thought about what it would mean for Kimiya.

But, now this. Perhaps his *nafs*, those hissing serpents, controlled him after all. Perhaps his love of Shams *had* blinded him, as the Brothers accused. Had he made a terrible mistake?

Dropping down, he lets his forehead touch the rooftop. He places his hands beside his head and prays with renewed earnestness, as a wet pool forms beneath his beard.

The moon rolls overhead twice before he hears the rooster crow. When, at last, he reaches for a copy of the Koran and opens it randomly, he sees reads: "No one has his life prolonged and no one has his life cut short except as it is written in a book of God's decrees."

185

47

What appears to you as a setting
  is for me a rising.
What appears to you as a prison
  is for my soul an endless garden.

During the mourning period, Aloeddin cannot bear to be at home, where his innocent sister met death. He wanders alone on the outskirts of Konya, heartsick and bereft, pondering his situation. Before the uncouth Shams arrived, the world made sense. His father was the beloved *sheik* of the community, so he, the son, had purpose and direction. His father was the center, and he revolved around him.

But after Shams showed up, his father grew deranged. Now Rumi's eyes, once clear and sober, appear intoxicated. His face, once serene, has twisted into a stranger's face. Even his heart seems to belong to another time, another place.

It is a true son's duty to rescue his father from madness, even to force him to see the error in his ways. *I must try one last time to remind him of who he is, of his duty to the family, to the Brotherhood, and to the Shar'ia. To the man he was before Shams.*

Coming home after two weeks with his purpose renewed, Aloeddin enters the reception room and bends his knee to kiss his father's hand. His lips brush the rough knuckles. Rumi bows his head and, for an instant, their eyes meet. To Aloeddin, Rumi seems momentarily to recover himself and to recognize him with tenderness.

Then the tapping of Shams' staff on the floor intrudes. Tap, pause, tap, pause. *The dervish dares to return during the mourning period!* His father's eyes glaze over, and Aloeddin feels invisible again.

Shams speaks muffled words, something about going to Salaoddin's house. And Aloeddin flees, the door slamming shut as he moves out into the streets in wretched confusion. *If I don't know my father, I don't know myself. If my father's identity is illusory, then so is my own.*

Without thinking, he finds himself turning down the lane toward the mosque. A leatherworker heaves under the weight of a tooled saddle on his shoulder. A scholar in black robes carries an armful of books as he scurries away. Aloeddin does not see himself as a scholar like his father, writing *fatwas*, analyzing al-Ghazzali and Ibn Arabi. He does not see himself as an obedient disciple like Velad, who follows the Master silently like Jami, the cat. And he certainly does not see himself as a mad lover of God like the interloper, flying here and there in search of a spiritual confidante while wrecking havoc in communities of pious Muslims.

I should learn a trade: carpet weaving, stone cutting, cooking, ah, cooking. . . . But just as quickly as the thought comes up and brings with it a moment of pleasure, he shuts it down. *No, I am a man of God, whose life centers around the law and the Koran.*

Aloeddin still carries within him that gentle boy who longs for his mother and never wants to leave the pungent smells of the kitchen. The man, Aloeddin, senses that boy at times when he is around the women cooking or the children playing. But near the men he becomes more serious, more religious than the others.

Yes, he is part of a great family, but it is time for him to distinguish himself. *I will be respected, and my name will be remembered in years to come. People will say that I belonged to the path of righteousness, that I saved them from the madness by restoring their law and their hope.*

Aloeddin never speaks these thoughts aloud. Nor does he speak them to himself exactly. They are vague feelings that lie dormant inside him. But Omar, Mehmet, and Iqbal whispered a plot that is awakening them. And, as a result, they are gaining strength with each passing day.

Those men need me to achieve their goal, to give their cause the righteousness it deserves. I will teach that dirty fakir *not to monopolize*

Rumi's time, not to ignore the obligatory duties. I will drive him away and become a hero to my people.

When Aloeddin reaches the mosque on top of the hill, he scans the city below. *That Shams is the source of all the trouble. Maybe he is a hypnotizer. . .maybe he is uncircumcised. . . . The biggest heresy of all: Shams told father to place trust in* him *rather than in God. Oh, false prophet!*

When he tries to conjure up Rumi now, his father recedes – and the intruder grows larger and larger, darkness snuffing out the light.

Omar is right. Something must be done.

48

Don't be fooled –
The short-cut to the king's house
  is a thousand miles out of the way.

Shahid tosses about like straw in the wind, squeezing his eyes shut to cover his terror of flickering shadows on the wall. Trying to calm down, he tells himself that his mother can hear his pleas. But his racing heart keeps him awake until the summons to prayer.

As the voice of the *muezzin* fades, he drops into a fitful sleep and wakes up drenched in sweat. *I missed dawn and morning prayers! What will become of me?*

A full two years has gone by since his initiation, and he has achieved nothing. Since that first taste of the garden in the Master's presence, he has had no spiritual experience. He remains the same lonely boy he always has been. *And Kimiya took with her the promise of an end to my loneliness.*

The mourning time for Kimiya is now past, and it is time for action on her behalf. Shahid steps outside. The air is shrouded with mist, so he cannot see far ahead of his footsteps. He moves noiselessly, his head bowed, his long legs lurching ahead of his body.

He hoped that, on the day of this meeting, the road might open beneath his feet and clear a way for him toward his noble aim. But the same dirt clods trip up his sandals. He hoped that a censer of incense might show him the way. But he smells only sheep.

He stops, about to turn on his heels and circle back. *Why trust these angry men with hard hearts?* He sighs. *Because I am one of them.*

Continuing toward the mosque, his breath comes rapidly. *The Master must know we will be meeting. He knows everything. And God, who is all-seeing, all-hearing, and all-knowing, He must know what we do here.*

Arriving, he sits in a prayer niche, his heart thumping. Suddenly, the patter of footsteps grows louder. *Will the angel on my right shoulder note my actions as good? Will the angel on the left record them as evil?*

49

The smell of apples arises
 from the orchard of my soul.
One whiff and I am gone –
 toward a feast of apples
 I am going.

Later that night, inside Salaoddin's house, Rumi, across from Shams, stares intently at the chessboard. In a couple of moves, he will be checkmated. "Oh, I've lost," he pretends despair.

"No, you've won!"

Rumi chuckles as the dervish picks up the rubaab and plucks its strings, a melody filling the air with sweetness. Rumi rises and spins slowly and gracefully on his left foot. With each turn toward Shams, he feels like a bud turning to face the sun.

A loud knock interrupts him, and a harsh voice exclaims, "Shams of Tabriz, come and meet your destiny!"

Shams leaps to his feet, sending the rubaab flying across the floor, while Rumi stops turning in midstep. Shams grabs his shoulders firmly. He reaches out and grabs Shams' shoulders, squaring them off. The older man flinches, then his body yields to his fingers.

"I will always love you," Rumi thinks he hears Shams say. "I will always be with you," he hears in the silence of their touch.

A tall white candle flickers in the gloom. The banging on the door grows louder. Rumi releases his grip and crumples to the floor.

Shams mutters, "I vowed to give my head."

Rumi stares up, greedily taking in that face. He reaches out and, as Shams begins to cross the room, grasps his ankle. "No, not yet. . ."

"It's God's will, you'll see." He lifts off his pointed hat and places it beside Rumi. Then, rising to his full height, he leaves his staff leaning against the wall and, without looking back, advances through the back door into the moonlit garden.

Rumi jumps up and bolts toward the open door. The scent of night-blooming jasmine rushes toward him.

He pulls the door shut to close himself in against the scents and sounds of the night. To close himself in against the despair, against the moment they knew would come.

Picking up a cushion, he presses it against his chest. *Maybe Shams will outwit his enemies again. Of course, he will outlive them all!*

50

I appear as a steady mountain.
Yet bit by bit,
toward that tiny opening
I am going.

A slice of moonlight shines down on Salaoddin's house and garden. The dark tent of sky is covered with clouds blocking out the stars.

Five dark-robed men circle Shams tightly, a flock of crows, their murmurs like feathers rustling. Shams raises his hands to the sides of his head and Shahid makes out, "*Allah, allilah*" as a dagger enters the dervish's chest.

Iqbal catches him from behind, under the arms, as his head falls back, then flops forward. The flaming eyes meet Shahid's for an instant. Gagging, he throws his glance onto the ground, where red puddles form in the cracks between the cobblestones.

Mehmet drapes a dark robe over the body, and Omar stoops down to cinch a rope around the ankles. All is silent.

In unison the men carry him, a shapeless sack of grain, to the well behind the house. Lifting him up, they drop the body down into the dark.

Shahid hears the water gurgle as it receives the weight. He scans quickly, left to right, but the others have flown, leaving a criss-crossed map of muddy footprints.

From within, the sounds of Rumi wailing.

51

Had everyone sought God
instead of crumbs and copper coins,
they would not be sitting on the edge of the moat
in darkness and regret.

Omar stretches a long arm around Aloeddin's shoulders and secrets him away toward his own *medrasa*. They move through the dark city as nocturnal animals, encircled in darkness, Aloeddin shuffling behind, a lost stray.

When they arrive, Omar's Brothers are waiting in the obscurity around the courtyard fountain for news of that dervish who humiliated their *sheikh*. As they approach, the men grow still, staring at him.

Omar breaks the silence. "It is done."

"Praise Allah!" A short, stumpy man raises his arms upward. "The infidel is gone."

"You are the heroes of Konya," claims another who strides forward to embrace Aloeddin in a tight grip. "Because of you, our city will return to the old ways."

"Not only Konya!" Omar adds. "Tomorrow I leave for Baghdad to fight the *jihad* in that great city. Praise Allah and goodbye to you all."

Aloeddin gulps in a breath, his eyes burning, and turns away from them, exiting the courtyard and entering the night alone.

Shahid sits in his cell alone, a white skullcap on his head, a thin coat over his muslin pantaloons. Unceasing thoughts pound him like waves slapping a shore. Reaching over, he lights a small taper, which casts an animal-shaped shadow on the wall.

He feels chilled to the bone, his limbs trembling, his teeth rattling. As he sways in silence, his hands twist around one another as if to wash something away.

The waves of despair stop rushing in as his mind empties after the storm. Nodding, he falls off the edge of the waking world.

A slice of moonlight shines down through a misty starless night onto a stone well. Suddenly, dark-robed men appear, barely visible against the gloom, forming a tight circle around a white gown. The sound of feathers rustling can be heard. Then a loud groan rings out and "la ilaha ill'Allah" splits the air. Water gurgles.

"Shams, Shams!" Shahid screeches as his left arm flails and knocks out the little candle. Gloom envelopes him. Disoriented now, he dreads sleeping as much as waking. Eyes opened or closed, the same murky vision appears.

Fervently, he pleads, "I seek the forgiveness of God for myself and others. I ask God to purify me from the effects of my wrongdoing," over and over, without knowing how his lips move.

But he gets pulled back down into the foggy night. Again the well appears. The moon, the body, the blood . . . . He wakes up, gasping for air.

Who am I? Just a man who wanted to be loved? Or a raging beast who kills by nature?

He loves Kimiya, that much he knows. And her marriage and death could not have been God's will. No, they were Rumi's will.

And yet he loves the Master too, so fiercely that Rumi's love for another inflamed him to blood lust.

Now I am an infidel born of that love. Shahid has admitted to himself everything but that, everything but the fate of his soul. *Now I can never be purified, not without the grace of God Himself. I must repent.*

His mind races: He wants to tell everything, but he is sworn to silence by his Brothers. They vowed to let their hearts become the graves of their secret. But another part of him is compelled to tell the truth.

The very questions he avoided asking all his life haunt him now. *Who have I been striving to please? What is the burden I have been carrying like a stone? When can I finally rest?*

A walled fortress within him crumbles, and his greatest fear comes forward like a specter. *If I reveal the truth, I will end up alone forever.*

Once again, Shahid slips from the world of light into darkness. Moonlight shines down on a stone well. Dark-robed men lift a white-robed body and drop it down a well. Water gurgles.

"Shams! Shams!" he screams himself awake.

At his morning ablutions, Shahid looks down at his hands. Once he begins to wash them, he cannot stop. He rubs and rubs until the skin is red and raw.

Later, when he enters the seminary, the sounds and smells of the place offer no refuge. He is no longer a part of the orderly rhythm of prayers, the melodic chanting of *zikhr*. So, he wanders about in an endless desert of the mind, Kimiya's face his only oasis. Retreating to a prayer niche, he gazes at her and feels what it means to adore. She peers back at him, and he feels cherished. She calls out to him, and he feels chosen.

Returning to his cell, he stares at the blue robe, then at the shoes made just for *sema*, then at the Koran in a wall niche. Each object is a reminder of who he is not. *From now on, every pious act – kissing Rumi's hand, offering charity to a widow, fasting for Ramadan – will be a lie to cover up my real nature: evil.*

Just outside his door he hears Rumi's familiar footstep. A faint hope of redemption arises in him. *I must go to the Master now, confess my part, and surrender to my punishment, letting Rumi's forgiveness wash away the filthy feelings.*

He starts toward the door but stops, immobilized. The terrible secret binds him to silence after all.

52

Why take bitter medicine for the ills of your heart
when the sweet water of love fills the world?

When the hot rays of morning spill purple onto the sky, Aloeddin heads home. Dervishes of many orders mingle in front of his house, stifling their whispers. As he approaches, they clear a path to the door.

Rushing to his room, his head low, he begins to roll a Koran and a caftan into a small carpet. But, before he can get away, Kira peers in. "You must go to him," she commands, indicating that Rumi is up on the roof.

He wanted to avoid this confrontation but realizes with resignation that he cannot. His whole body shaking, he climbs the ladder. As he steps onto the terrace, his father, facing the hills, turns toward him, his mouth set tight, his eyes wild.

"No!" His father's cry is piercing.

What does he see? Does he look into me? Aloeddin follows Rumi's glance down. The hem of his robe is smattered with blood.

"Father, I. . . ." He closes the distance between them and bends his knee, reaching out for Rumi's hand.

But his father backs off, pointing the long index finger of his right hand at him, as his stern voice rings out, "You will answer for what you have done. As the Koran says, 'the hard of heart will be in blazing fire.'"

His father pauses and, in the pregnant stillness, the life drains out of Aloeddin.

"You are no longer my son. I don't ever want to see your face again."

53

This is love – to fly upward
toward the endless heavens.
To rend a hundred veils at every moment.

During the next few weeks, Rumi refuses work and becomes as listless as a mendicant. He refuses food and becomes as thin as Shams' staff. He refuses to dance, a current of grief wrapping itself around him.

Beneath the protective dome of the mosque, which shelters him from the glaring dome of the sky, he crouches on a prayer carpet, his hand clutching his heart.

He is convinced that his beloved avoided his fate and evaded his foes as before. Whatever heinous act Aloeddin and those other defiant Brothers attempted in the garden, Shams must have tricked them too. He must be breathing the same air that he breathes here now beneath the dome. The same air that warms his nostrils, fills his chest, and circles through his blood. *Yes, I am certain. Shams is breathing it too, somewhere nearby.*

Or he is back in Damascus beating someone at chess. That's it. More likely, he did not stay in Konya and is in Damascus again.

Restlessness pushes Rumi out of the mosque and through the streets toward the city gates. *I will get confirmation of Shams' whereabouts and send Velad. No, I will go myself in search of Shams, that minaret in whose body the air circles, call us to prayer.*

Drifting through the streets, oblivious to the streams of people coming and going, he reaches the edge of the city when a sugar caravan arrives. Approaching a textile trader in a woven caftan, whose bales are piled high on a wagon, he accosts him without the greeting of peace, "Where is Shams? Have you seen Shams of Tabriz?"

The trader pulls back, shaking his head in wary silence, and moves to protect his goods.

Frantic, he runs up to a wizened old man who leans on a stick. "Where is the caravan leader of souls? Have you seen Shams of Tabriz?"

"No, Master, I don't know the man."

Rumi's heart sinks. But he holds onto his conviction that Shams is alive as he rambles back into town.

Turning a corner at the entrance to a lamp shop, Rumi comes face to face with a merchant. "Have you seen the Sun, Shams of Tabriz?"

A gnarled face beneath a soiled turban answers, "Yes, Master, he is in Damascus."

Rumi shrieks with joy. Removing his robe and lifting the turban from his head, he hands them to the astonished stranger.

Arriving home, he rushes to tell Velad the news. His son sets down the book he was reading, his mouth frowning. "No, father, it's not true. Shams is gone, and so is Aloeddin."

Rumi falls onto a cushion, his heart splintering into a thousand pieces. His bare head in his hands, he mutters, "I gave my gown and turban for a lie. But I would have given my life for the truth."

54

I don't belong here.
I am not a candle,
I am a wisp of smoke.

At the next evening call to prayer, Shahid crouches at the fountain, sweeps wet fingers over his face, rinses his mouth, nose and ears, and stares at his hands. Holding them under the stream, frantic, he rubs and rubs them, the skin already tender and raw. *Be still, hands, you are clean now.* But they wring and rub each other without rest.

That night he dreams that he sits beside the Master in the reception room as golden light casts shadows on the floral walls. Rumi places his palm on the back of his hand. The Master's hand has been refined by the touch of hundreds of sacred books. Or perhaps the ninety-nine names of God traveling through his breath to all parts of him have soothed even this, the palm of his hand. Until it sits so still on him that it quiets even *his* hand, stopping the fear from rumbling through him. And he enters a moment of presence: nothing to repent, just Rumi's large, still palm on his knuckles.

Then it lifts off, and his own hand sits there, alone again. And his mind begins to buzz like a hive.

Shahid awakens with the fierce conviction that he must go to Rumi now. *A Sufi is a son of the moment. I should not put this off until tomorrow again.*

He wants to tell him his life story: how his father left, his mother left, then his love for Kimiya, and she is gone too. And his love for Rumi, and how he felt when he left him for Shams. He just wants to tell him everything, to confess his lack of faith in God. And how all of it led to that gruesome moment in the garden. He wants to take his life and wrap it up in a bundle and place it at Rumi's feet.

Quickly dressing in his blue robe and *sema* hat, he rushes from the seminary down the road to Rumi's rooms, where he receives permission to enter. Standing outside the reception room, he waits. From behind the curtain he hears Rumi and Velad whispering urgently. And then that word, that unmistakable word – murder!

He freezes, a ghostly chill running through him.

Rumi is telling Velad, "A murderer is one who takes life, so he should be called the son of the angel of death, Azrael, whose 4,000 wings all have eyes. His son can only take life – that is his fate."

My confession is pointless. I can never be forgiven now. I have to run, like Iqbal and Mehmet, and live without a Master, alone.

He removes the tall, felt *sema* hat from his head. The hat he made with his own hands. Bending down, he sets it on the carpet.

"If his heart turns in repentance, he will be forgiven by God and God alone," Rumi mutters on the other side of the curtain.

Like a shadow, Shahid slips out the door.

55

O flute, you have no tongue, yet you wail all day.
For whom do you cry?
They took me from His sweet lips,
What else can I do but cry?

As Rumi burns for Shams, Kira burns for Rumi. One evening at dusk, she wanders aimlessly like a beggar through empty rooms, seeking remnants of him. She picks up his old leather slipper, wrinkled and worn with traces of his daily pilgrimage to the mosque. *A rarefied mind, the gritty scent of mud on his feet.*

As darkness surrounds her, she approaches the pedestal candle where he used to stand taking his follower's questions or reading philosophy. When she lights the wick, and the flame flickers, she feels that she enters his private world, and a startling image arises in her mind: Christ on the cross, his hands bleeding. Christ, anointed and abandoned. Sacrificing personal desire for something greater than himself. Sacrificing the law for love.

Rumi is Kira's dying God. The man she learned to worship as a child and the man she adores as a woman share the same longing and the same fate – God consciousness.

She returns to her own room and lies down on her mat. Her mind quiets, her jagged breathing evens out as she rests for a while, at the edge of sleep. But soon she startles awake and sits bolt upright: *Rumi's Judas is his own son.*

Three weeks after Shams' disappearance, her husband returns from one of his wanderings, crossing the threshold into the kitchen like one possessed by a *jinn*: his eyes flitting about, his arms flailing at nothing, his tongue speaking nonsense. It seems to Kira that he, like Shams, has passed into another world.

After he retreats to his room, she tiptoes in to bring him a tray of food. The odor of stale sweat hangs in the air. He sits cross-legged on the bare floor with Shams' pointed hat in his lap. With his left hand he holds the hat still. With his right, he runs his fingertips over the points, caressing them tenderly. When he twists around to face her, she hardly recognizes him: the stringy hair, the sunken cheeks, the savage, haunted eyes.

Panicking, she rushes to the courtyard to find Velad. "What is the difference between this despair and insanity? He runs from life to some other world where he sees his dervish and dances with him. He wails like a babe and rants like a madman. Perhaps we should send him to the asylum where they play music to ease deranged people."

"Mother, it will be alright. He gives himself up to Allah. He will return to us, God willing."

But Kira is not so sure. She is beginning to imagine the worst.

56

Lovers of truth – rise up!
Let us go toward heaven.
We have seen enough of this world,
*   it's time to see another. . . .*

During the precious hours when others sleep, Rumi climbs to the rooftop terrace. He forgets the sight of the glistening moon. He forgets the sound of *zikhr* circling back like a hawk. He forgets the sensation of his head in the dirt, sweet surrender.

He stays up for the dawn, but the new light does not dispel his darkness. Instead, he broods. *Some are baptized in fire. I am baptized in grief. Tears, my ablutions.*

Standing up to leave, he does not know who made the decision to stand. Bowing and kneeling in the position of prayer, he does not know who made the decision to kneel. *I am controlled by something outside myself. God is thrashing through me, snatching me up and casting me down again.*

Just then, in a kneeling position, his body seizes. He tries to move but cannot. A searing pain grips the base of his spine. White heat shoots up his back into his head and out the crown, opening a window in his skull. Misty vapors rise and connect him in a stream of light to the heavenly light above. The air fills with the scent of wisteria.

Someone opens the door. "Father, are you alright?"

It must be Velad. "Stay by me, son. Don't abandon me now."

Velad steps nearer as he gets up, lifting his arms and crying to the skies, "I live between contraction and expansion. In grief, the door is closed on the face of the Beloved. Nothing holds the water of life. Nothing calls me to break the silence.

"In ecstasy, I see only the face of Him. Nothing without the water of life. And despite these words, the silence is never broken." He pauses.

"One minute, a sorrow so dark and bottomless. Next minute, a light so bright." *These words, so needed and so inadequate.*

"One minute, a separation that cannot be bridged. Next minute, a connection that cannot be broken."

After forty days, Rumi gives up hope and dresses in mourning robes, a dark, ankle-length skirt, a yoke-collared white shirt that stretches to his thighs, and a black waistcoat over them. He rips open the shirt at the chest, dons a new honey-colored cap, and wraps it in criss-crossed patterns with a purple-black turban. Finally, he slips on yellow leather sandals.

Stepping into the garden, he places his right hand around a post and begins to turn, lifting like a wing. All of his life prepared him for this final turn. His body has been hollowed out by fasting, his mind emptied out by chanting the names of God.

Whispering the *zikhr* al-Fatah, the One who opens the treasuries of His mercy for His students, he leans into the movement slowly at first, then faster and faster. Beneath his hand the post disappears. The garden dissolves, the dirt, the sky. He gives himself up to the whirling until he is nothing but whirling. And verses, swift and startling, pour out of the spinning robes:

> *Let us go,*
> *bowing to the ocean*
> *like a raging torrent.*
> *Let us travel from this desert of*
> *hunger and tears*
> *to the feast of newlyweds.*
> *Enough with these forms!*
> *Let us go to the Formless One.*

Dancing on the lip of insanity, he moves through the things of this world with their own motion – turning. As he whirls and vanishes, whirls and vanishes, he becomes still inside.

Now let us be silent
so that the giver of speech may speak.
Let us be silent
so we can hear Him calling us
secretly in the night.

When the moon rises in its fullness, Rumi leaves the garden and returns to the rooftop. He is beginning to realize that his spiritual exile is nearly over. Homecoming is here.

In his first separation from Shams, a poet was born. That longing, that burning for the beloved gripped him and drove the poems out of him. But desire remained – desire for *him*.

In this separation, he dies even to *that* desire. His gaze turns inward toward the brilliance of a million suns.

Weeping on his threadbare prayer carpet, he can see it now: Shams' death was with him from the beginning, ever since he began to love him. In the first tap of his staff, in the first embrace of his arms.

He could not have become illuminated if Shams had lived. Shams *had* to vanish. With his death, a new life dances in Rumi. With the heavens turning above and below, he hears a secret in his ear: "Die before you die."

I am dying to Him, for Him, in Him. This surrender, this dying to separation is Him after all. This death, a second birth.

This is the final boundary of his life, the rung of the ladder that was there waiting for him. Through the many years of yearning, he came near to Him, just two bow's lengths away. Now, even that short distance is closing.

From the roof he can see out over the dirt streets and narrow alleys to the minaret, which sparkles with light. It does not reach up to heaven. *Heaven is here and now.* His prayers do not fly up to heaven, to be caught by God's hands. *No. God is here, now, praying through me.*

Letting his head fall back and his mouth yawn open, he cries, "Praise Shams. Praise God. *Mas'Allah!*"

Praising God brings him such relief. This grief was, after all, only the handmaiden of praise. This winter of grief summoned him to the springtime of praise. Shams diffuses into the air, a fragrance that pervades all things.

God's name sweeps over the grassy plains, making the reeds dance. His name lifts the birds' wings, moves through tiny lungs, and sings in their song. It hums in the bees as they circle the nectar and in the cries of the *muezzin* as they circle the tower. His name turns the earth in the heavens – and the dervish on the earth.

All is holy. The flute calling to the reed bed, the homing pigeon circling back, the infant suckling at the breast. I am in them, they are in me, all part of the great return.

When the sun peeks out behind the horizon, he climbs down the ladder into the passageway. And Shams looms up, misty looking, thin and filmy. The air about him trembles. He holds his massive staff in one hand, a candle in the other. He raises his right hand with the tiny candle. A circle of light spreads around him.

As Rumi approaches, Shams sets down the candle and places the same hand on his heart. His body thins into mist and is gone.

57

We sing of heart, soul, and the Beloved –
Only to burn all trace
      of heart, soul, and Beloved.

The following week, Rumi strolls through an orchard on the outskirts of town among shy buds and trembling leaves. His devoted disciple, Husamoddin, moving with his square chin jutting forward and his long nose slightly in the air, is at his side. Spring has painted the countryside in ruby red, soft pink, and deep violet. He pauses to finger a tiny white blossom with a gold center, its life short and fragile, its gift a great beauty. Gray clouds dance over distant peaks.

That flower, those clouds, they are not separate from him now. His heart reaches out and wraps itself around them, as if they too are a part of himself, a part of God. He feels the promise of rain through his skin, bypassing his nose, eyes, and ears, and entering him directly. His skin has thinned like the horizon where heaven and earth meet.

As the sun cuts through a cloud, the disciple breaks the silence. "Master, I have heard your verses burst forth and vanish into the air. I have witnessed them touch a man's mind or a woman's heart, then be gone. But they might change minds and melt hearts for years to come. I can see people in the distant future becoming intoxicated on their wine -- if we write them down."

Rumi reaches up to his dark purple turban and pulls out a torn sheet, nodding at Husam. "I will call it The Mathnawi, a step-by-step journey toward home. Let's begin."

> *Listen to the song of the reed,*
> *how it wails with the pain of separation:*
> *'Ever since I was taken from my reed bed*

my woeful song has caused men and women to weep.
I seek out those whose hearts are torn by separation
for only they understand the pain of this longing.'

Reciting it aloud, Rumi realizes that the reed stands for Adam, the first man. Only in his exile from Eden did Adam begin to make art. *Only separation fires the imagination. Only separation ignites this creative life. Another gift from Shams.*

The next day, Rumi invites the disciples to join him for sunset prayers at the new *medrasa*, which has just been built by Sultan Jelaluddin Karatay. He hurries through dried grasses, past sun-baked houses beneath a hazy, gray sky. As he approaches the *medrasa*, the dome's triangular turquoise, black, and white tiles glisten in contrast to the surroundings.

Pausing beneath the arched doorway, he steps out of his shoes and enters the hall for the first time. The prayer niche is covered with cobalt blue tile. The walls are decorated with knotted script, scrolls, and arabesques in white on gold, which change to an inlaid pattern of blue interlinking stars on the dome's curves. The top of the dome opens to the sky, which is turning from blue to black. He sighs with pleasure, as the stars twinkle to life above him. In the center of the floor, the starry sky sparkles too in a small pond.

Their eyes wide, the Brothers stand around in awe. He must instruct them quickly. "This sanctuary is not what you seek. The holiness of the human heart – that is the real mosque. The moment we proclaim His name, the domes and minarets disappear. He alone remains."

The *muezzin* calls them to the highest realization. Lining up, the men lift their hands beside their heads and praise God in one voice, his breath joining theirs. Together, they lower their hands to their hearts and sing the opening chapter of the Koran, as they descend deeper into contemplation, their minds stilling. Resting their hands on their knees, they whisper like lovers to the beloved. After bending, they fall to the floor in submission, kissing the words, "Glorious is the supreme reality." Drawn back into a seated position, they rest, then fall forward again in total abandon. Crying *"Allahu akbar,"* they are resurrected in standing position.

All eyes turn toward him as he turns more fully toward Him, gliding to an open area, lifting his right foot, and spinning on his left. His arms outstretched, his head slightly tilted, the spinning pulls him down and in as the walls disappear, the stars vanish. His body moves without effort, without friction, as his mind empties into silence. Even his breath is gone.

Hovering like a cloud, he recites,

The man of God
  is drunk, but drinks no wine;
He is full, but eats no meat.
The man of God
  spins with ecstasy,
  and doesn't care about food or sleep;
He is a king beneath a simple cloak,
a diamond amidst the falling ruins.
His wisdom
  is born of the supreme truth,
  not from the pages of a book.
  He is beyond faith and doubt,
  he knows not right or wrong.
The man of God
  has bid farewell to Nothingness
  and has returned in all his glory.

58

What is your life about?
Nothing but a struggle to be someone,
Nothing but a running from your own silence.

At dusk, a messenger arrives at Rumi's house. Aloeddin's twisted body, half covered with dirt and leaves, was found by a traveler on the road to Laranda. His soiled white turban lay by his side, his carpetbag gone. The traveler realized that Aloeddin's patched robes were those of a dervish and carried the body in his cart to the local *sheikh*, who identified him as his son.

Aloeddin must have been going toward or returning from the grave of his mother in Armenia. He sends the messenger back to retrieve the body and, on his return, finds out that Iqbal and Mehmet fled there with him.

Late that night, on the rooftop terrace, Rumi repeats aloud the evening prayer known as the black light. As his mind returns from afar to the sensation of the carpet beneath his knees, the direction of his prayer changes.

"God forgive Aloeddin, I ask God to purify him from the effects of his wrongdoing. God forgive Aloeddin, for I cannot."

He can forgive the infidels, who do not know the ways of Allah, the merciful and compassionate One. He can forgive Mehmet for his demons of jealousy and anger. He can even forgive Shams, who stepped out to face his destiny with God's name on his lips. But he cannot forgive his son, who became as stiff as a dried up branch that is disconnected from its stream water, with no inclination to sway.

Two days later, as the community gathers to bury and mourn for Aloeddin, Rumi is unable to participate. He wants to mourn alone. Proceeding toward the gardens of Meram, he passes thatched huts where geese and ducks waddle through the yards. Black-veiled mothers hang out white fabrics on ropes to dry. At a cattle herder's camp, a scrawny old woman holds a goatskin bag, fills it with milk, and shakes it, waiting for the cream to form.

He sits down among the gold and orange nasturtiums and prays again, silently begging God to forgive Aloeddin. *He lost his mother at such a young age. And his father. Did I neglect him for my duties? for Velad? And then Shams . . . .*A single tear forms and slides down into his beard.

But Aloeddin was not like him or Velad. He did not long for a direct experience of union. He clung to beliefs. He did not enter the path of love. He defended the law. And yet. . . *he was my son.*

Suddenly exhausted from his reflections, Rumi gets up and goes toward Husammoddin's empty house, a small mud-brick hut on the edge of the gardens. There, he drinks a glass of tea, stretches out on a carpet to rest, and falls into a dream.

Shams' silhouette appears at the top of a knoll, the pointed hat and long staff standing out against the sky. Aloeddin comes up from behind the hill and appears beside him in brown robes. His son kneels to kiss the beloved dervish's hand, his head bowed low. Shams grabs Aloeddin's shoulders, raises him up, and embraces him.

Rumi wakes up with a start, his breath rushing through him as a wild river. *Shams forgives him! Of course. . . Aloeddin was his instrument.*

Rushing out the door, he runs through the gardens and down the hill toward the grave of his son.

59

Once you taste the wine of union,
what will be your faith?

As the next day's brightness pushes through the dark curtain and filters onto the rose-colored carpet, Velad sits beside his father in Aloeddin's room to say a silent farewell. As Rumi turns within, Velad takes in the scene. A bare wall with a large whitened square where a carpet once hung. A few small rugs scattered about. A water jug on its side on a threadbare sleeping mat. No books in the wall niche.

People said that Aloeddin read nothing but the Koran. Velad feels barren, like the room.

As he joins the meditation, his heart is quelled. When he opens his eyes several hours later, his father radiates serenity. He is no longer a tormented man longing for his Beloved, no longer a thirsty man striving to taste the divine. Velad wants desperately to understand what has taken place within his father.

After a few more minutes, Rumi inhales, rubs his hands on his thighs, and lets his lids open to the daylight. "I hear the questions of your heart, Velad. I know you want to understand my journey now."

How does father know my heart and mind like that?

"You see," Rumi continues, "I have been like a piece of cloth dipped into a vat of dye that is the color of God. Over and over again. Until, finally, nothing else remains. I am that color. I am the Sun. I am God."

Shivers go up Velad's spine. *It's forbidden! No mere man can be God. That is heresy.*

"Knowledge is different in different stations," his father says. "Until I reached this level of intoxication, I didn't know what the martyr Mansur Hallaj meant when he spoke those blasphemous words of union with Him – I am God. His sober listeners heard a great pretension, a cry of spiritual pride. But there was no heresy in him -- humility itself was speaking. He had transcended himself. He was nothing. God was all."

"Then why did Hallaj die on the gallows, father?"

Rumi breathes close to his face. "That death was a prerequisite to life. I too have died, becoming a drop in the ocean. And in this death is my life."

60

O heart, what a wonderful bird you are.
Seeking divine heights,
> *flapping your wings,*
> *you smashed the pointed spears of your enemy.*

1259 A.D.

The breeze carries the scents of spring through Konya to the prayer lodge, where morning sunlight heightens the colors of red and blue in the carpets. Rumi is instructing a new student in how to begin a meditation retreat before taking the vow of allegiance. An unknown dervish, in the green robes and turban of another Order, waits near the door until he sends the novice, with a *sema* hat in hand, off to his cell.

"*Asalaam,*" he greets the dervish, pointing to a cushion.

"Master," the man speaks tentatively, "I know here the empire seems to be at rest like a sleeping beast. But nearby the Mongols and Christians have formed an alliance in their holy war against us."

More alert now, Rumi nods toward his guest to continue.

"In Damascus, three Christian princes entered the city as conquerors, to the horror of believers there. In Baghdad, the hordes slaughtered more than a million and a half believers, assaulted thousands of our chaste women, and turned the world's largest library into a heap of ash. The Tigris and Euphrates ran with blood, and the last sultan of Baghdad, prince of the faithful, was choked to death. And now Samarkand, Kaiseri, and Aleppo have been ravaged as well."

Aleppo, Rumi remembers it well. Years earlier he witnessed the Shia displaying their grief on the anniversary of the death of Hoseyn, grandson of the Prophet. They wailed, thumping their chests with their fists and whipped themselves into a frenzy, blood spilling down their faces and onto their torn shirts.

With this memory comes a shocking realization. *I no longer spurn the Shia. I am no longer concerned with differences among us. In fact, I no longer consider myself a Muslim.*

He takes a breath, and something releases deep inside him. *I am a lover of God, and those who follow me, Muslims, Christians, or Jews, we are a nation of lovers. Our religions divide us, but our yearning for God, our* himma, *unites us, whether we are Muslims longing to join Allah, Christians longing to be embraced by Christ, or Jews yearning for the Messiah.*

In his inmost heart, Rumi thanks God for the revelation and mourns all of the dead, regardless of their beliefs.

"Will we flee the invaders, Master, or fight them in *jihad*?"

The guest's question intrudes on his reflection. Long ago, his father's decision was to run from the invaders. *And now?*

During the next few days, the infidels' tents crop up around the edges of Konya until a whole small village of white triangles dots the land. A few errant Mongol intruders break into a family's home, steal their bread, and raid their vegetable garden. Stunned neighbors stand by, too frightened to protest.

Then a band of invaders gallops through a cemetery on the outskirts of town, smashing headstones and desecrating the burial grounds. Rumors spread of a Mongol horseman killing a boy for his goat. A few families panic and depart for Egypt, where the Mameluks offer refuge.

In the reception room beside Velad, Rumi broods. *The Mongols are here. What is their vision of paradise? What are the names of their God, who drives them to massacre and burn and destroy?*

Praying for guidance, he beseeches Him to help him make the right decision to protect Konya. And, suddenly, he knows what he must do. Shams' message so long ago to the Shia *imam* comes back to him now.

"Velad, our task is not to purify the world of those we call our enemies. Our task is to purify the inner world of hatred – to cleanse

222

the soul of inner enemies. That's the hidden meaning of fighting evil for the sake of God."

In his new spiritual station of union or *baqa*, he feels no fear. "I am going to meet the infidels, Velad. I will make *jihad* in my own way."

"No!"

His son's disobedient word startles him.

"Don't go alone . . . ." Velad's plea fades as he hurries purposefully through the door.

Velad rouses himself and rushes out to follow his father. He does not believe that he can alter Rumi's course, yet he must try.

In the streets, a gust of wind blows debris about everywhere. Men and women hasten to pack a few things while their children wait in carts. He dashes past a Christian monastery, and the woody fragrance of incense wafts by. A black-robed monk, in bare feet, crosses himself as he observes the exodus.

Searching for his father, Velad spies him climbing the rubble hills and reaching a clearing on the summit. Running until he is out of breath, he catches up with Rumi and falls onto the scrub, panting. The outline of his father's body is silhouetted against the sky. A celestial light shimmers around his robe. *But it is only the flashing rays of the golden midday sun.*

As Rumi raises his palms to the sky, the birds overhead stop wheeling and fly off. He closes his eyes and takes air into his chest, but there is no in. And there is no out. His breath is smooth, effortless. Nothing separates him now from anything else.

The earth trembles beneath his feet. He opens his eyes as hundreds of charging horses appear out of nowhere, stampeding toward him from all directions, carrying troops of men in fluttering black capes with square faces and almond-shaped eyes. They advance quickly, their bows and arrows already drawn.

Just then, he hears a whisper in his ear, "Do what is needed. Your actions are rooted in God the Exalted. Your will and His will are one."

The infidels pull back their bows all at once. Arrows fly like swarms of hissing insects rushing this way and that. But they do not pierce him. Instead, repelled by an unseen force, they go off in all directions.

Again, in unison, the invaders lift their bows – but their hands cannot draw them back. One of the commanders yells and shakes his fist in the air. Defiant, he reaches into his quiver for an arrow, aims, and shoots straight at him. But, instead of hitting him, the arrow spins back toward the shooter and clatters at his feet.

The Mongol soldiers shout in alarm, pull their steeds around, and gallop away in retreat.

Rumi is filled with gratitude. "God is great!" His praise echoes through the hills and up into the heavens.

I am not of wind or fire
    or of the stormy seas.
I am not formed out of painted clay.
I am not even Shams of Tabriz –
I am the essence of laughter,
    I am pure light.
Look again if you see me –
It's not me you have seen.

-- Jelaluddin Rumi

Time Line

600-800s Rise of Muslim dynasties in Arabia, Egypt, Syria, Spain, Afghanistan, No. India

800s and 900s Small groups of mystics practice *sama*, musical recitations and dance, to the horror of sober Muslims

922 al-Hallaj put to death for claiming "I am God"

950s Turks of Central Asia convert to Islam

1050s Seljuk Turks enter Islamic territory and take Baghdad

1071 Seljuks take Rum (Greek/Roman territory, including Turkey today)

1096 The 1st Christian Crusade takes Jerusalem

1100s Sufi mystical communities, under the obedience of a single *sheikh*, begin to emphasize direct communion with god over obeying the Shari'a or Muslim law

1116 Seljuk capital established at Iconium/Konya

1147 Second Crusade

1152 Muslims recover Jerusalem from Crusaders again

1187 Saladin retakes Jerusalem and removes the cross from the Dome of the Rock

1204 The 4th Crusade takes Constantinople.

1206 Temuchin takes the title Genghis Khan. Sultans take Northern India.

1207 Rumi is born in the area of Balkh, which is now northeastern Afghanistan, to Sufi *sheikh* Bahaoddin

1215 St. Francis's order of friars begins to preach love and poverty

1217 Crusade against sultan of Egypt fails.

1218 Genghiz Khan conquers Persia.

1219 Rumi's family and several hundred disciples of Bahaoddin flee the Mongols and the town leaders, who turned against Sufis

1220 Balkh is reduced to ruins by Mongols, who also take Samarkand and Bukhara

1220-1237 Reign of Aloeddin Kaykobad

1219-1225 Rumi and family travel in exile through Nishapur, Baghdad, Mecca, Damascus, Aleppo, Laranda (now Armenia), where his mother died.

227

1224 Rumi marries Gevher Khatun

1226 Rumi's first son, Sultan Velad, is born in Laranda

1227 Death of Genghis Khan, whose sons launch expeditions in Arabia, Persia, Turkey

1228 Rumi's second son, Aloeddin, is born. The 6th Crusade.

1229 Sultan invites the family to Konya, Turkey

1230 Gevher dies, Rumi marries Kira

1231 Bahaoddin dies, Rumi takes his pulpit at age 24

1240 Rumi's teacher, Burhanoddin, and philosopher Ibn 'Arabi, die

1240-1244 Rumi teaches traditional religious law, gains followers, and recites his Discourses

1242 Seljuk state becomes Mongol protectorate; Mongols force sultan of Konya to pay tribute

1244 Shams arrives in Konya, stays one year and three months.

1246 Shams disappears and Rumi grieves, reciting his 50,000 verses of

Divan

1247 Shams returns to Konya, marries Kimiya, and is murdered

1248 The 7th Crusade. Louis IX enters Egypt

1249 Rumi becomes the spiritual friend of Salaoddin, marries Velad to his

Daughter

1252 The Church crushes heresy with torture in the Inquisition

1256 Rumi begins to recite his greatest work, the Mathnawi

1258 Baghdad falls to the Mongols and Muslim rule ends under the Caliphate (except in Egypt)

1259 The fall of Damascus and Aleppo. The Mongols take China.

1259 Rumi saves Konya

1260 The Mameluks of Egypt defeat the Mongols, turning the tide.

1261 Rumi recognizes Husamoddin as his successor

1273 Rumi's wedding with the Beloved

Acknowledgments

Omar Kaczmarczk, Dear One, who opened the door and changed my life;

Fariba Enteshari, lover of Mevlana, who lit the way by translating Farsi texts and sharing hours of *sohbet*;

Ernest Luddy and the Luddy Family Foundation, whose generous support put the ground beneath my feet;

Jonathan Star, who graciously offered his translations to adorn the text;

Marina Budhos, who handed me the first compass in a new land;

Phoebe Larmore, who joined me in the new land, exploring it line by line, breath by breath;

My writing group -- Pami Bluehawk Ozaki, Marsha de la O, PK Candaux, Karen Gottlieb, and Mary Jane Roberts -- whose honest critique and support were indispensable;

My giggle group – Neil, Linda Novack, Rhoda Pregerson, Riley Smith, Steve Wolf, Paula Perlman, Janet Bachelor, Bruce Langhorn, Malcolm Schultz – brothers and sisters whose love and laughter sustained me through it all;

Aaron Kipnis, dharma brother, whose friendship and feedback nourished me like food;

Cheryl Yates, for layout, formatting and technical assistance that made this book possible;

Candice Fuhrman, whose fierceness forced me to hone my craft;

Coleman Barks, Kabir Helminski, Andrew Harvey, Shahram Shiva, Nader Khalili, and others who have lived with Rumi's teachings and brought them to a larger audience;

Postnesshin Celaluddin Loras, whose gracious hospitality in Turkey was a teaching. Thank you for opening the Turn to women;

Sunlight and Ruminations, internet sites whose messages brought daily inspiration and resources;

Anne Marie Schimmel, Reynold Nicholson, and A.J. Arberry, whose scholarship and translations are a great legacy;

Jonathan Lewis, Sheikh Iqbal, whose early contributions helped to get me going;

Ibrahim Gamard, who shared his expertise;

Russell Galen, whose comments led me down the final stretch;

Friends who gave precious time to read the manuscript in loving support: Bob Forman, Andra Akers, Linda Bloom, Susan Taylor Chehak, Naomi Lowinsky.

The best for last: Neil, Cher, Sage, Mike, Tina, and Jane for the love and the longing in my heart.

Permissions

The author gratefully acknowledges permission to reprint translations of Rumi poetry by Jonathan Star. Used with permission of the translator, Jonathan Star, from:
A Garden Beyond Paradise: The Mystical Poetry of Rumi (trans. Star and Shahram Shiva), Bantam Books, 1992.
RUMI: In the Arms of the Beloved (trans. Star), Jeremy P. Tarcher/Putnam Books, 1997.

About the Author

Connie Zweig, Ph.D., is a Jungian-oriented therapist and spiritual counselor in private practice in Los Angeles. She has been a student of the mystical teachings and practices of Hinduism, Buddhism, and Sufism for more than thirty years. Former columnist for Esquire and contributor to the Los Angeles Times, she is co-author of the best-selling Meeting the Shadow and Romancing the Shadow. Her work on illuminating the dark side of human nature has been featured nationwide. She is also author of The Holy Longing: The Hidden Power of Spiritual Yearning, which explores the psychology of religious aspiration and the shadow side of spiritual and religious life. She has taught around the country about human spirituality, religious abuse and disillusionment, and shadow-work. A Moth to the Flame: The Life of Sufi Poet Rumi is her first novel. It is the inner story of holy longing as lived by Sufi poet and teacher Jelaluddin Rumi.

Dr. Zweig can be reached at www.conniezweig.com or 310-285-8453.